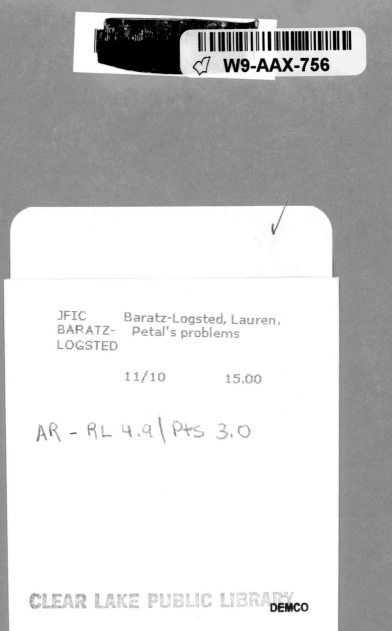

THE Sisters 8

BOOK 6

PETAL'S PROBLEMS

By Lauren Baratz-Logsted
With Greg Logsted & Jackie Logsted
Illustrated by Lisa K. Weber

sandpiper

HOUGHTON MIFFLIN HARCOURT
BOSTON • NEW YORK • 2010

The text of this book is set in Youbee.
Book design by Carol Chu.

Library of Congress Cataloging-in-Publication Data
is on file.

ISBN 978-0-547-33402-8 paper over board
ISBN 978-0-547-33403-5 paperback

Manufactured in the United States of America
RRD 10 9 8 7 6 5 4 3 2 1
4500252473

For Lucille Baratz,
a.k.a. Mom, a.k.a. Grandma

Annie   Durinda   Georgia   Jackie

Marcia   Petal   Rebecca   Zinnia

PROLOGUE

"Oh no! The sky is falling!"

"Oh no! It is raining so hard! What if it rains for forty days and forty nights?"

"Oh no! If the sky falls and it rains for forty days and forty nights, not only will we be orphans, we'll be drowned orphans, dead with the sky crushing our heads!"

"Oh no—"

Sound like anyone you know?

Of course it does.

And you know a lot of other things too. Really, you know all the basics at this point.

Powers. Gifts.

Annie: power—can think like an adult when necessary; gift—purple ring

Durinda: power—can freeze people, except Zinnia; gift—green earrings

Georgia: power—can become invisible; gift—gold compact

Jackie: power—faster than a speeding train; gift—red cape

Marcia: power—x-ray vision; gift—purple cloak

You also know, because you've been paying good attention, that at the end of Book 4: *Jackie's Jokes,* a flock of carrier pigeons thundered into the home of the Eights bearing notes that said, *Beware the other Eights!*

You also know, because you have a pretty decent memory, that at the end of Book 5: *Marcia's Madness,* an invitation arrived announcing the wedding of Martha Huit and George Smith on Saturday, June 21, 2008, and cordially requesting the presence of the Eights . . .

In France.

Honestly, you know so much, you don't need me to tell you a great deal more.

But one thing you don't know, can't possibly know, is that a strange event has happened in the world of the Eights. You know that each sister's adventure occurs within the space of a month. Annie's was January; Durinda's, February; Georgia's, March; Jackie's, April; Marcia's, May. So it should be Petal's turn and June now, right? Only the thing you don't know is that it's not. The Eights are still stuck in May, looking at that invitation and wondering what's to be done about it.

This state of affairs is perfectly fine with Petal. Why, as far as Petal is concerned, it could stay May forever, for all of eternity. You see, Petal doesn't *want* June to come.

But it really doesn't matter what Petal wants, does it? Time can't be stopped. So even if it's not quite June yet, it must inevitably come. And when it does, it will be time for . . .

Oh no! Petal power!

To which, all I can say is . . .

Ha!

ONE

e've been invited to a *wedding?*" Durinda said.

"In *France?*" Rebecca said.

"And who, by the way," Georgia said, "are Martha Huit and George Smith?"

"Don't you remember," Annie said, "our relatives Aunt Martha and Uncle George, who used to come visit us occasionally?"

We supposed we'd always known about these people. We dimly remembered that Aunt Martha thought that everything made her look fat, and Uncle George liked to cook but was very bad at it, which meant we had to lie so as not to hurt his feelings. But we didn't know anything about them beyond that, plus we hadn't seen them in so long that, frankly, we'd forgotten all about them. And anyway, we'd learned to be suspicious of relatives. So, we thought as we narrowed our eyes in suspicion, who were these people really?

"Is it just me," Marcia wondered aloud, "or does anyone else feel like it's supposed to be June already . . ."

"I'm glad it's not June!" Petal cried. "I hope that wretched month never comes! Perhaps time has stopped, or even started running backward? But oh no! What if it *is* running backward and it keeps on running backward? Eventually, I will be a baby again and then *gulp!*—after that I will cease to exist!"

"But I don't understand." Jackie was puzzled. was also ignoring Marcia and Petal, as were we all always thought Aunt Martha and Uncle George we from the same side of the family—you know, broth and sister."

"Oh," Zinnia said wistfully, ignoring nearly everyone and everything. "I would like to go to a wedding. I'm fairly certain they have lots of presents at those."

"Apparently not." Annie answered Jackie, ignoring Zinnia. "The invitation specifically lists them as Martha *Huit* and George *Smith*." She shrugged. "So I guess they're not from the same side of the family, not brother and sister at all. If Aunt Martha is a Huit, she must be Daddy's sister, and if Uncle George is a Smith, he must be Mommy's brother."

"Who knew?" Jackie looked stunned.

"Apparently not us." Annie shrugged again. "Anyway, now it looks like Daddy's sister is marrying Mommy's brother."

"My, we *do* come from an odd family," Rebecca said, a dark gleam entering her eye. Some of us found that disturbing, how rather pleased Rebecca appeared at the thought.

"So what are we going to do about the invitation?" Durinda asked Annie.

Since Mommy and Daddy's disappearance back on New Year's Eve, Annie had taken over as head of our household. It fell to her to make all the important decisions, like what to wear to Will's birthday party or when would be the best time to change the oil in the Hummer. But some of us thought that in this particular instance—this particular instance being what to do about an invitation to a wedding in France—it shouldn't be left up to just Annie. Some of us thought it would even be a good idea, the *best* idea, to put it to a vote.

Too bad for some of us then.

"We have to say no, of course," Annie said simply.

"But why?" some of us shouted.

In this instance, *some of us* equaled Georgia, Rebecca, and Zinnia. The first two were always up for an adventure, and the third loved the idea of going anyplace where there might be presents, even if those presents weren't for her.

As for the rest of us . . .

Annie had already made up her mind.

Durinda was content to let Annie decide.

Jackie wasn't the shouting type.

Petal was too grateful it was still May to be bothered with anything else.

And as for Marcia . . .

"But it is supposed to be June, right?" she said, perplexed for once. "Honestly, am I the only one to notice that there's something wrong here?"

"But I want to go to the wedding," Zinnia said, a tear threatening to spill over the edge of her eyelid. "Even if it's in France, I want to go."

"Don't you see, though?" Annie said gently. "That's part of the problem. It *is* in France."

"Annie's right," Petal said, finding something fresh to worry about, even though she'd just been told it was never going to happen because, according to Annie, we were *not* going to the wedding. "We can't go to France! We'd have to swim there! And if we tried to swim all that way —wherever France is—we would drown!"

"Well, no," Annie said, "we won't drown."

"Of course we'd drown!" Petal barreled on. "How could we not drown? We will—"

"We won't drown," Annie said, beginning to lose patience, "because we won't be swimming."

That stopped Petal in midpanic. She was stumped. "But if we don't swim, then how would we get there? I'm fairly certain France is not right next door . . . is it?"

"Of course it's not." Rebecca sneered at Petal, then turned to Annie. "Is it?"

"Well, it could be," Annie said. "But whether it's just a country away or a continent away, we wouldn't swim to get there. We'd fly."

"Oh no!" Petal clutched her head as she began running in circles. "This is even worse than swimming! We can't fly like birds!"

"That's funny," Rebecca said, studying Petal as she ran faster and faster. "You're doing a pretty good job of it. Any second now, you might really take off."

"We won't swim to France." Annie was getting more exasperated by the minute. "And we won't fly like birds either. We'll take a plane."

"*Aiyeeee!*" Petal cried. "That's the worst idea you've come up with yet!"

Zinnia crossed one arm over the other and then

swept them apart, like an umpire making a call at home plate. "Can we all just ignore Petal for a moment?"

"Gladly," Georgia said.

"Do you have something to say, Zinnia?" Durinda asked.

"Yes," Zinnia said, extreme if cautious happiness entering her eyes. "Did anyone else hear what I just heard?"

"You mean Petal losing what's left of her tiny little mind?" Rebecca said.

"But that's nothing new," Georgia said. "She loses what's left of it practically every day."

"I didn't mean that," Zinnia said, growing more excited still. "I meant Annie. She said, and I quote, 'We'll take a plane.' She was talking in the present tense. That must mean we're going to the wedding. We're going to France!"

We all turned to Annie, wondering. Was this true? Even Petal stopped running in circles long enough to look at her.

"'Fraid not," Annie said, answering our questioning looks with a rare blush. "That was just a slip of the tense. I meant that's how we'd get there if we *were* going, which we most definitely are not."

"Thank the universe!" Petal said, collapsing into a happy, exhausted heap.

"But why not?" Zinnia, the most disappointed among us and the last to hold on to any shred of hope, said.

"Because it is in France," Annie said. "Because we would have to fly there and we would need passports, which none of us have."

We didn't?

"Well, do you?" Annie demanded.

Sadly, we shook our heads. It would be nice to be international travelers, people of mystery and intrigue like James Bond 007, but that wasn't us. Even Mommy and Daddy always said it was scary enough just taking us across state lines.

"No," Annie said with a satisfied nod of the head, "I didn't think so. On top of *that* problem, there's the even bigger problem of what we would tell people."

"How do you mean?" Durinda asked. She may have been willing to go along with whatever Annie dictated, but even Durinda secretly longed to go to the wedding.

It would be so much fun. It would be *different*.

We liked different. Or at least most of us did.

"It's like this," Annie said. "Whenever we have to explain to nosy parkers why Mommy and Daddy aren't around, we always say—"

"That Daddy is in the bathroom and Mommy is in France," Jackie cut in, beginning to see what Annie was getting at.

"Or vice versa," Georgia added. "Sometimes we say it the other way around. It's good to have variety, mix things up a bit."

"And that's the problem," Annie said. "How can we go to the wedding of Aunt Martha and Uncle George—Daddy's sister and Mommy's brother—*without* Mommy and Daddy? How could we ever explain their absence on such an occasion? Obviously, we can't say that one or both of them are in France because—"

"Because the wedding is *in France*," Zinnia finished, thoroughly getting it and thoroughly glum now.

"Exactly," Annie said gently.

"So what do we do?" Durinda asked.

Annie sighed. Sometimes she seemed like Atlas, trying to hold the weight of the whole world on her shoulders. Some of us thought that it could get pretty heavy, but only occasionally did Annie appear to mind. And even then, we suspected that her appearing to mind was just for show.

She studied the invitation again.

"They've included a reply card," she said at last. "It says to RSVP no later than June seventh." She handed the card out toward Durinda. "You'll take care of this for us?"

"Of course," Durinda said, reaching for the card, but before she could grab hold of it, a smaller hand snatched it.

"May I do this?" Zinnia asked timidly. "I know it's not the kind of job you'd usually entrust to the youngest—you know, the importance of RSVPing and all—but I am so sad we are not going to the wedding, I think it would make me feel just the slightest sliver better if—"

"Say no more." Annie patted Zinnia on the shoulder as another tear threatened to overspill Zinnia's eyelid. "If it makes you feel better, of course you can be the one to RSVP no for us."

"Really, people!" By now Marcia's hands were on her hips. "Doesn't anyone else think this is all too strange?"

We all stared at her. What *was* she going on about?

"*June?*" Marcia tapped her foot impatiently. "Isn't it high time for it to be *June?*"

* * * * * * * *

And then it was June.

First it was June 1, a Sunday, and then it was June 2 and time to go to school.

But one of us was nowhere to be seen.

So we searched for Petal and found her in the first place we looked.

Petal was under her bed.

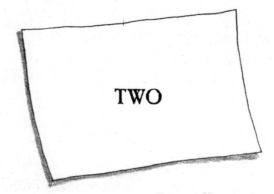

TWO

June had always been a sweetbitter month for us. It was sweet because it meant the end of another school year and graduation into another grade—yay! summer vacation!—but it was also bitter because the end of another school year meant being separated from our classmates for most of the summer. We would miss those classmates. Or at least we'd miss Will Simms. And maybe we'd even miss Mandy Stenko, a little.

This June was no different in that regard.

But this June *was* different, because Petal wouldn't come out from under her bed.

"The bus will be here any second," Durinda informed Petal gently.

We were all crouched down, peering under the bed, trying to get Petal to come out.

"If we miss the bus," Georgia pointed out, "we'll have to call Pete for a ride and that hardly seems fair. You know he does have to work for a living."

"I won't come out! I won't come out!" We heard Petal's muffled shout.

"You have to come out sometime," Marcia said, reasonably enough. "You'll need to eat."

"Durinda can shove my meals under the bed," Petal said. "I'm never coming out! Or at least, not until July first."

"There are only two weeks of school left," Jackie said. "If you don't go to school for two weeks, you won't graduate with our class. And then you'll have to stay behind next year, all by yourself, and have the Mr. McG again."

"I'll take my chances," Petal said with a rare burst of bravery, however misplaced. "But I'm not coming out! I'd rather stay under here with the cobwebs. So long as I never have to get my power, I'll be happy."

We sighed. Had there ever, in the history of the universe, been an Eight who wasn't eager to get her power?

There had not.

But there was one now.

"But if you never get your power," Zinnia said, "you'll never get your gift, because that's the order these things usually happen in. Well, except for Georgia. Sort of. Don't you want your gift?"

"No!" Petal shouted so loud, her voice didn't even come out muffled this time. Really, our evil toadstool of a neighbor the Wicket could probably hear her just fine next door.

"This is getting ridiculous," Annie muttered.

"Hmm, desperate times," Rebecca mused. Then she raised her eyebrows and looked at Annie with a hopeful expression. "Desperate measures?"

Annie straightened to a standing position, gestured with her hand at the bed. "Be my guest."

Rebecca grabbed hold of Petal's ankles and pulled her out from beneath the bed in one swift yank.

Unhappy, Petal rose to her feet and brushed the cobwebs from the skirt of her yellow plaid school uniform.

"Fine, I'll go to school," Petal said, "but it's under protest."

"Works for me," Annie said.

Petal gestured at the bed with her chin and glared down at Rebecca from her one-inch advantage in height. You'd think that after nearly eight years of living together, we'd be used to it by now, but it was always a shock to realize that Petal was in fact taller than Rebecca. Mostly, it seemed like Petal should be the smallest of us, even smaller than Zinnia. As for Rebecca, even though she was the seventh in terms of birth order, there was something timeless about her, and sometimes she seemed even older than Annie, older than the world.

"I can do this every day," Petal informed Rebecca.

Rebecca tilted her head up an inch to meet Petal's eyes, then she flexed her yanking fingers. "So can I."

* * * * * * *

So that's how the first of the last two weeks of school passed for us, at least in the mornings.

"I won't go! I won't go! You can't make me!" from Petal.

Then would come "Oh yes, you will!" followed by a yank from Rebecca.

And then we'd go off to school for the day, where the Mr. McG would continue trying to teach us new things, even though a hint of summer was already in the air, making it hard to concentrate, and at recess we'd play in the yard with Will Simms, and even Mandy Stenko.

* * * * * * * *

Then Saturday came.

It started the same way Monday through Friday had, with Petal under the bed.

Apparently, Petal had gotten into a rut.

"It's not a rut," her muffled voice informed us. "It's common sense. I can just as easily get my power on a weekend day as on a school day, and I don't want it."

"Oh, bother," Annie said.

"Can't we just leave her like that over the weekend?" Rebecca said, rubbing her wrists. "This whole process every day—it's fun doing the yanking, but I am getting sore."

"'Fraid not," Annie said. "This weekend we need to do spring cleaning, and Durinda can't be expected to do it all by herself."

"Spring cleaning?" Georgia looked appalled at the very notion.

"But spring started on March twentieth and summer begins on June twenty-first, the same day as Aunt

Martha and Uncle George's wedding." Marcia looked puzzled. "Spring is almost over."

"Exactly," Georgia said. "See, Annie? You've left it too late, so there's little point in doing all that work now only to have the season end in two weeks, so why don't we just—"

"Get working." Annie cut her off. "Why don't we all just get working?"

"But Petal has to come out and do her share," Zinnia said. "If one of us doesn't do her share, then it's like getting an anti-present for the rest of us."

"You know, though," Jackie said, not using a mean voice at all, as some of us would have if we were the ones to say this, "it's not like Petal does her share even when she actually does anything." She shrugged. "So

would it really make any difference if we just left her under there? I mean, she does seem happy . . ."

"Of course she has to do her share," Annie said, "even if she doesn't really do anything. It wouldn't be fair otherwise. Rebecca?"

Rebecca flexed her sore wrists and with a weary sigh took hold of Petal's ankles.

"C'mon, Petal," she said with a great yank. "Can't spend your whole life under a bed."

* * * * * * * *

So that's what we did, spent Saturday cleaning under Annie's direction, because that's what Annie wanted us to do.

We put on our sloppiest clothes, which made Georgia very happy and Rebecca even more so, and each of us slapped a babushka on her head to keep the dust off.

We had thought of those pieces of cloth simply as bandannas or kerchiefs folded in a triangle shape, but Jackie informed us as we worked that the proper word was *babushka* and that it was Russian.

And oh, did we work!

We dusted and polished and swept and scrubbed and cleaned and scoured.

Even our eight cats got into the act. At first, Anthrax, Dandruff, Greatorex, Jaguar, Minx, Precious, Rambunctious, and Zither were reluctant to join in. They didn't like getting their gray-and-white-puffball paws dirty unless it was their own idea to do so. But when Durinda made a tiny little babushka for each of them, they seemed to like the fashion accessory so much that they really got into the spirit of things, tidying up their own cat room and pitching in with the four seasonal rooms.

Given the strict cleaning regimen Annie had us on, we would have liked to go to Summer, Fall, or Winter—really, anything but Spring—but Annie wouldn't have it.

"Come on!" she encouraged us. "Whistle while you work!"

"Whistle while we work?" Rebecca, covered from head to toe with soot from cleaning out all the chimneys, a job for which she'd eagerly volunteered, raised a withering eyebrow at Annie. "Surely you must be joking."

But it was no joke doing all that cleaning.

Did we mention that we dusted and polished and swept and scrubbed and cleaned and scoured?

We worked so hard that day. Even Petal kind of worked. And none of us tried to shirk her duties except when Zinnia asked for a five-minute break in mid-afternoon.

"Where do you need to go for five minutes?" Annie asked mildly.

Really, it was just a casual question, like asking people how they are that day or what the weather's like where they are or what they had for lunch. Even Rebecca couldn't find any fault with that mild question.

But Zinnia did, reacting oddly.

"Why do you want to know?" she demanded. "Who are you, the Grand Inquisitor? I have to go to France! Or maybe I have to go to the bathroom! Is that okay with you? And what are you, anyway, some sort of slave driver? Sheesh!"

And then Zinnia disappeared for exactly five minutes.

It really did seem odd to us, her behavior, but when she returned, she looked so much happier than when she'd left, we all thought it best not to say anything.

By the time the late spring sun had started to set, we'd put in a full day, and our home was cleaner than it had been since Mommy's disappearance. Not that Mommy had ever done much cleaning. She was an important scientist, too busy with her inventions to bother with such things herself, but she did know whom to phone to come do the cleaning for her.

And it sure wasn't robot Betty, the robot Mommy had invented to make our lives easier but who never did.

As we surveyed our newly clean home, we sighed. Our day would have been so much easier if before Mommy had disappeared to wherever she'd disappeared to with Daddy, she'd thought to leave us the number of whoever it was who did all the cleaning for her.

Just then the doorbell rang.

"Can someone get that?" Annie shouted when no one did. "I am still busy here."

Annie was standing on a small stepladder polishing the facemask of Daddy Sparky, the suit of armor we used to convince nosy parkers that our real daddy was still at home. Annie had already fully dusted Mommy

Sally, the dressmaker's dummy we used to fool people into thinking our real mommy was still at home.

"It's Mr. Pete," Zinnia announced cheerily, holding on to Pete's hand as she tugged him inside.

Pete was our favorite mechanic in the whole world.

He gave a low whistle as he surveyed the room. "This place looks fantastic_

We blushed.

"But what are you doing here?" Annie said, coming down off her stepladder and wiping her hands on a rag as we all gathered around. "I didn't mean to be rude, but I didn't call you for help with anything . . . did I?"

"Of course you didn't call," Zinnia laughed nervously. "But isn't it great that he just popped in like this, unexpected? Why, we can just tell him what we've been up to lately, fill him in on every little thing and—"

"What are you talking about?" Pete the mechanic looked down at Zinnia, a confused expression on his face. "I'm not unexpected. You called me this afternoon and invited me over."

"So *that's* where you were!" Annie pointed an accusing rag at Zinnia. "You joked that you had to go to France. Or at least I thought it was a joke. You said you had to go to the bathroom."

"Oh, come on." Rebecca rolled her eyes. "When is any member of our family actually in France or the bathroom when we say we are?"

"But see," Pete said, "that's why I'm here."

"Huh?" all of us except Zinnia said.

"What's this nonsense I hear?" Pete said. "You lot have been invited to a wedding in France—*France!*—and according to Zinnia, you're not planning on going?"

THREE

Annie paused just long enough to shoot a sharp glare Zinnia's way before launching into an explanation of why we couldn't go to France.

When she was finished, Pete was silent for a long minute, stroking his chin.

We waited, some of us patiently, some of us breathlessly.

"Let's see if I've got this straight," Pete finally said. "The way I see it, you've got two reasons not to go. One, you've no passports. Two, you have no reason to give for your parents' not being there, since you can't say they're in France when you are, in fact, in France. Have I got that right?"

"Pretty much," Annie admitted.

"So if we could solve those two problems," Pete said, "you'd go?"

"Well, yes," Annie said, but then she started to

hedge. "But then other problems might present themselves too, so who knows?"

"Well, let's tackle these two first before we invent any new ones," Pete said, "shall we?"

"I don't want to go to France," Petal said. "It's my month, and I don't want to go. Why, I don't even want to get out from under the bed in the mornings!"

Pete blinked. "Did she just say out from *under* the bed?"

Seven heads nodded.

Pete blinked again. "You don't all sleep under your beds, do you?"

Seven heads shook, vehemently.

"Well, that's a relief then," Pete said. "I was getting worried that maybe you'd all gone crazy."

"No," Rebecca said. "Just Petal."

"Yes, well," Pete said, "we can deal with that later. Now, getting back to your first problem: passports. But see, that's not a very big problem at all."

"Of course it is," Annie said. "We probably need an adult to go with us to get them. I mean, the passport office doesn't usually just hand out passports to kids on their own, does it?"

"If it did, the world would be chaos!" Petal said, horrified.

"And aside from that," Annie went on, ignoring

Petal, "there are only two weeks left until the wedding. So even if we could get a nice adult to go with us to the passport office—like *you,* say—I'm sure the passport office doesn't move that quickly. It's a bureaucracy, and believe me, I know all about working with bureaucracy. Its wheels grind slowly."

"They do," Pete admitted, "for normal people. But I know a man who knows a man who . . . Put it to you like this: we'll just snap a few pictures of you lot, and then I can get this taken care of for you in no time. You'll get your passports."

We looked at Pete, stunned. He wasn't just a mechanic; he was well connected. The man was a miracle worker!

"But wait a second." Annie narrowed her eyes. "This sounds fishy: a man who knows a man who . . . Are you sure this is legal?"

Thankfully, Pete didn't take offense. He simply shrugged. "If it's not, it should be," he said. "You're eight little girls who want to go see some relatives get married. You should be able to do that if you want to, even if it's in France. There shouldn't be any laws keeping you from leaving the country. I mean, it's not like you're criminals." He paused, thought about that one for a bit. "Are you?"

Eight heads shook.

"Well, I sort of am," Annie admitted, timidly for once.

"*You?*" Pete's eyes widened. "What have you done that's criminal? Robbed any good banks lately?"

"No," Annie said, "but I do forge Daddy's signature on checks and when I pay with his credit card. I also forged his name when I signed his tax returns in April. I'm fairly certain all those things are against the law."

"Details." Pete waved his hand dismissively. "You only do those things out of necessity. You'd never do it if you didn't feel you had to in order to survive." He paused again. "You wouldn't, would you?"

Annie shook her head, clearly outraged at the very thought.

"There you go then," Pete said. "So, okay, we've got the passports covered, or will soon enough. But this problem of what to say about why your parents aren't with you . . . I have to admit, that *is* a big problem."

"Yes," Zinnia said seriously as she placed her hand on Pete's arm. "But I have faith in you. You'll solve it."

"Hmm . . . can't say they're in France . . ." Pete thought, and then his eyes lit up and he snapped his fingers. "*I* know!"

"You *do?*" Georgia sounded shocked. And then we realized that Georgia didn't always have quite the faith in Pete that the rest of us did, certainly not as much as Zinnia.

"Why, yes," Pete said, "it's so simple. I don't know why none of us thought of it sooner."

"But since you *have* thought of it," Rebecca said grumpily, "you can tell the rest of us anytime now."

"You just need to say to anyone who asks," Pete said, "that your parents had to stay home, that your father had a big modeling job locally and your mother had an important new invention that was keeping her close to home as well."

Huh. That had never occurred to us. We could simply go, now that Pete was arranging for our passports, and then say Mommy and Daddy had to stay home for work purposes. No one would ever question the importance of the work of a model or an inventor/scientist.

"But we don't have a present to give them," Annie said.

Pete looked at Annie wryly. "Didn't take you long to come up with another excuse not to go, did it?"

"It's not an excuse." Annie blushed. "But you do need to bring a present when you're going to someone's wedding, don't you?"

"Oh yes!" Zinnia said. "A wedding—any celebration, really—is not complete without presents."

"I hate to admit it," Rebecca said, "but they're right. We would need to bring a present, and I doubt we would find one at the Grand Emporium of Children's Delights."

"That's our favorite store," Jackie put in.

"It's the only one we've ever gone to on our own in order to buy someone else a present," Marcia added.

"It was grand there," Durinda said. "And it was definitely an emporium. A delightful one, actually."

"I wish we could go back." Zinnia sighed.

"It's true, you would need to bring a present," Pete said, "and Rebecca's right, I don't think you can get an appropriate one at that store you mentioned."

Rebecca's right—those weren't words you heard around our house every day, certainly not together.

"But there's an easy fix for that one too," Pete went on. "The missus would be happy to take you. In fact, I can't imagine anything she'd like more."

The missus was what Pete called Mrs. Pete. We liked her. In fact, if our own mommy never came back, we'd seriously consider her for the job. Not that Mommy could ever be replaced. But Mrs. Pete loved us and was kind to us. She didn't even dislike Rebecca or Georgia, and she hardly noticed when Petal fainted. Honestly, she'd do in a pinch.

Pete looked at Annie, amused now. "Go on, pet. Make up another problem."

"I'm not making them up." Annie looked frustrated at the unfair accusation. Then her eyes lit up. "The RSVP! We can't go because Zinnia has already RSVPed no! I'm right, aren't I? You can't say no to an invitation and then turn around and say, 'Oops, sorry, I really meant to say yes. How did I ever get those two words confused? Silly me!' Right? You can't say that."

"Well, not like that, no," Rebecca said. "'Silly me'? Who talks like that? You'd sound like an idiot!"

None of us wanted to say so, but once again, Rebecca was right. That would be an idiotic way to put it.

"Oh," Pete said. "You already RSVPed no?"

"Yes," Annie said. "Zinnia said she'd do it."

"I didn't know that part." Pete's face fell. "I'm sorry. I guess this has all been a waste. Since you've already formally said no, you can't—"

"Um, about that RSVP," Zinnia cut in with a pained smile.

"Zinnia Huit!" Annie rounded on her. "Don't tell me you never RSVPed? But that's so rude!"

"Well, I was hoping—" Zinnia started to say.

"Hope all you want to," Annie said. "But the RSVPs were due back by today, June seventh, remember? It's too late now. Oh, this is just great. We never RSVPed and now we've missed the deadline. Our relatives will think we're rude."

"Well, Serena's crazy," Rebecca said, referring to our former substitute teacher who we later found out might be a relative of Mommy's, since at one point they'd shared the same last name, Smith. "Rude us, or some of our crazy relatives—who is to say which is worse?"

"Please, Annie," Zinnia said. "Can't we go anyway?"

"But what about the late RSVP?" Annie objected.

"So the RSVP will arrive a little late." Marcia shrugged.

"They'll still be happy to have us," Jackie said, "no matter how late our reply. I'm almost sure of it."

"You mean you both want to go too?" Annie said.

Marcia and Jackie nodded.

"I should like to go too, please," Rebecca said in the nicest voice we could remember her using in a very long time. She must have wanted to go very badly indeed.

"Me too," Georgia said. "I could use a spot of adventure. It's been a long time since I clawed my way out of that avalanche."

"How about you?" Annie turned to Durinda.

"Gosh, yes," she said. "I need to get out of the kitchen."

"But you could always go to the living room or any other room to do that," Annie pointed out. "You don't need to go all the way to France."

Durinda shrugged. "I'd still like to go."

Annie turned, finally, to Petal.

"And how about you?" Annie said. "If it's not unanimous, we won't go. Just say the word."

Petal looked at all of us. Poor Petal. She must have felt the pressure from all sides. It's a wonder she didn't pull out the miniature pink convertible Mommy had made and drive it around the inside of the house or put on her wall-walkers to climb the walls or her bouncy boots to bounce up and down, those being three things she did whenever she got too nervous about something.

We thought about that. In France, there would probably be no little pink cars or wall-walkers or bouncy boots to help calm Petal, but there would be plenty of people to hear Petal scream. It was not a pleasant thing to think about, so we stopped.

"Ohhhh, *fine!*" Petal screamed, cracking under the pressure. "I'll go to France! But I won't like it! I'll hide under my seat on the plane the whole way! Do we really need to take a plane? Can't we all just swim? And once we get there, I'll just go back to hiding under my bed, wherever my France bed might be! But *fine,* I'll *go.*"

"Yay!" We all started to cheer.

"But wait a second," Annie said.

"Oh no." Most people would never think to roll their eyes at Annie, but Pete did then, although he did it in a good-natured way. "She's thought of another reason not to go."

"Actually," Annie said to him, "it's your fault."

"*My* fault?" Pete's eyes widened.

"Yes," Annie said. "Your fault. That time back in April, when we were going into the Big City on the train to see Daddy's accountant, you went with us. You said you didn't think it was a good idea for us to go alone. Well, if it's not a good idea for us to go into the Big City without adult supervision, it can't possibly be a good idea for us to go to a whole other country!"

Pete opened his mouth to say something, but he was interrupted by a sound.

It turned out that the source of the sound was a carrier pigeon thumping against the glass of a window.

Durinda opened the window and let the pigeon in.

"Just one of you this time?" she asked, looking behind the carrier pigeon to see if there were any friends following.

We knew she didn't really think the carrier pigeon would answer her. Only Zinnia believed she could talk to animals and that they could talk back to her. We all, of course, knew different.

Still, we were glad to see the carrier pigeon was on its own. When your house has been thundered into by a giant flock of pigeons as ours had been back in April, each pigeon bearing the same disturbing message, you never look at feathered friends the same way again.

"What does the note say this time?" Petal asked fearfully as Durinda removed the tiny scroll from the metal tube on the pigeon's leg.

"Huh," Durinda said. "Well, would you look at that."

We all looked.

The note read: *Why not ask the Petes?*

We swore, sometimes these notes were like mind readers!

"Funny," Pete said. "I was just about to—"

"Will you?" Eight voices cut him off. "And Mrs. Pete too?"

"Yes," Pete said, "and yes."

FOUR

The second of the last two weeks of school passed pretty much in the same way the first had, at least in terms of the mornings, with Petal refusing to come out from under the bed and Rebecca needing to flex her sore wrists to yank her out. It began to appear to us that Rebecca no longer minded the pain. In fact, she seemed to be proud of it, even enjoy it.

"I'm not doing this for my health, you know," Rebecca would say when Petal refused to come out on her own.

"Could have fooled me," Petal's muffled voice would bark back.

"This is ridiculous," Rebecca would say. "You know there's no point in doing this. You already promised you'd go to France, so you'll have to come out on Monday, June sixteenth, anyway, when we leave for the plane."

"That is then and this is now," Petal would say. "As I keep telling you, the longer I spend under the bed, the safer I am—you know, less likely to get my power."

"And as I keep telling you," Rebecca would say, "that's the silliest thing I've ever heard. What, you think your power can't find you under your bed?"

"Perhaps I won't notice it or it won't notice me," Petal would say.

And then Rebecca would give her a good yank.

One thing was different that week from the week before. On Thursday after school, since the Mr. McG had for once assigned no homework, Mrs. Pete took us shopping for a wedding present for Aunt Martha and Uncle George.

And we did *not* get it at the Grand Emporium of Children's Delights.

Rather, Mrs. Pete took us to a place we'd never been to and had never intended to go to.

It was called the Super-Duper Razzle-Dazzle Bride-Groom Store.

"I hope the present is super," Zinnia said.

"I hope it's duper," Durinda said. She paused, looked puzzled. "Even though I don't know what that means."

"I hope it *rrrrr*azzles," Rebecca said, her eyes flashing as she rolled her *r* like she was speaking Spanish, a language the Mr. McG had begun to teach us since he said we needed to be bilingual in a brave new world.

Since we were leaving for France in four days, we did kind of think it would have been more useful for him to teach us French instead, but we did like that we were now able to count to ten in Spanish, and the *r*rolling thing was fun even if Rebecca tended to overdo it.

"I hope it dazzles," Georgia said.

"But how can we find one present that will make happy both a bride—" Jackie began.

"And a groom?" Marcia finished.

"I can't believe it," Annie said in a hushed voice. "Mrs. Pete drives that truck as good as Pete does. Why, she's almost as good a driver as me!"

For once, we ignored Annie. Sometimes we thought she was too obsessed with her own driving skills.

"*I* can't believe you all dragged me out from under the bed for *this*," Petal said.

Yes, it was true.

Despite Rebecca's rare common sense in pointing out that Petal's power could find her anywhere when it decided to descend, Petal had taken to hiding under the bed not just in the mornings but whenever we turned our backs on her for a second.

Annie had said that if she kept this up, we might have to get a leash for her. According to Zinnia, Precious —Petal's cat—was deeply offended at this.

What was also true was that the present we found was super; it was duper; it razzled; it dazzled; and we were almost certain it would be equally enjoyed by both a bride and a groom.

After all, who wouldn't want a Deluxe Perfect-Every-Time Hamburger Maker/Manicure-Pedicure Machine?

Okay, so maybe it wasn't as exciting as the Super-Duper Faux-Hockey Mash-'Em Smash-'Em Reality Toy Kit we bought Will Simms for his birthday back in January, but Durinda certainly thought it was fabulous.

"My days would be so much easier if I had one of these," Durinda said wistfully. "And my nails would look good."

The store even provided free gift-wrapping service, which was good since that wasn't one of our particular talents.

"It was so nice of you to help us pick out just the right present," Annie said to Mrs. Pete when it came time to sign the gift card. "Would you like to sign this too, since you're also going to the wedding?"

"No, thank you," Mrs. Pete said kindly. "Mr. Pete and I have already picked out a present to bring."

"Oh?" Annie was curious. "What did you pick out?"

"Cash," Mrs. Pete said. "People tend to like that too."

Huh. We'd never thought of that. And it would have been so much easier—so much less to carry on the plane!

Briefly, we considered keeping the Deluxe Perfect-Every-Time Hamburger Maker/Manicure-Pedicure Machine for ourselves—certainly Durinda did—but then Annie pointed out it wasn't in our budget to keep the present for ourselves *and* give a cash present, not when we were already spending so much money on plane tickets.

"Drat." Durinda snapped her fingers. "And I was beginning to look forward to perfect burgers—mine always come out shaped like hexagons—and pretty nails."

"You ought to try living under the bed like me," Petal advised. "Under the bed, no one cares what your nails look like. Really. And it's rather peaceful once you convince yourself that all those dust bunnies don't necessarily mean there are real bunnies about to attack you. In fact—"

"Oh brother," Rebecca muttered. "Sometimes I'm tempted to leave her under that bed forever. It'd certainly be quieter, and there'd be less stupidity floating around the universe too."

* * * * * * *

But the next day we couldn't leave her under the bed, as much as some of us would have liked to, because the next day was the last day of school.

Too bad it was also Friday the thirteenth.

"Oh, this is the absolute worst!" Petal cried. "It's worse than *death!* It's my power month *and* the last day of school is Friday the thirteenth? Oh, you can't possibly expect me to—"

Yank!

"I don't care how scared you are," Annie said. "It's our last day as third-graders—in September we'll be in fourth grade!—and we are *all* going."

* * * * * * *

The nice thing about the very last day of the school year is that it's a half day. Another nice thing is that it always feels like a Big Moment. Even if a person isn't having a major graduation, like from kindergarten to grade school or from grade school to high school, it still has that feel. Something is changing. Something is over and something else is beginning. It's like having your birthday. Once you turn eight, you can never be seven again, which is what would happen to us on August 8, 2008, but that moment in time was still in our future.

We, on the other hand, were still in our present.

"Before we begin having our last-day-of-school party," the Mr. McG announced, "I'd like to say how pleased I am with the progress you've made in the short time I've been your teacher."

Mandy Stenko raised her hand. Even though it was the last day of school and we were about to have a party, she was still raising her hand. Who does such a thing? Oh, right. She does.

"Yes, Mandy?" the Mr. McG said.

"Can you tell us who our teacher will be when we come back in the fall?" she asked. "It's just that I'm very worried. I heard that the very nice fourth-grade teacher has suddenly decided not to return in the fall"—and here, for some odd reason, Mandy glared at all of us—"and I'd really like to know who the new person will be. You know, so I can think about it all summer long."

"Sorry," the Mr. McG said, "but I can't give out that information. Besides, I don't want you to worry about school over the summer. I just want you to enjoy yourselves and have fun."

"Are you joking?" Mandy was shocked.

"Not at all," the Mr. McG said. He even smiled. Sort of.

"Can I come up there and feel your forehead?" Durinda asked.

"It's what Durinda does whenever one of us looks feverish," Marcia said.

"A *rrrrr*eally high feve*rrrrr* can kill a pe*rrrrr*son," Rebecca pointed out, rolling her *r*'s again.

"I am very scared of high fevers," Petal said. "The sniffles too. Those can be terrifying."

"I don't have a deathly high fever and I think I'd notice if I had the sniffles." The Mr. McG laughed. "I just think kids should enjoy being kids at the appropriate moment. Time and adult responsibilities will catch up with you soon enough."

Annie couldn't help but snort at this. Adult responsibilities had caught up to all of us to a certain extent when our parents disappeared—or died, as Rebecca would add—but Annie more so than the rest of us.

"Laze in a hammock," the Mr. McG suggested. "Drink lemonade. Lie on your back in a field and stare up at the puffy clouds, trying to see animal shapes in them."

"Or go to France," Jackie said.

The Mr. McG blinked but recovered quickly. "Or"—and here he waved his hand—"you could go to France."

"Then we don't need to study at all over the summer?" Marcia wondered.

"It would be nice not to," Georgia said.

"It would practically be like getting a present," Zinnia said.

"Don't be ridiculous," the Mr. McG said testily. "Of course you need to study over the summer, at least a bit, mostly math, so you don't lose everything I've taught you." Then his expression softened. "But other than that, your assignment is simply to be young. Be kids."

If he kept this up, we'd get all misty-eyed.

"Can we eat the junk food we brought for the pa*rrrrr*ty yet?" Rebecca asked.

Okay, so maybe one of us was in no danger of getting misty-eyed.

"Yes, Rebecca," the Mr. McG said. "It's party time. But you do realize, don't you, that you only need to roll your *r*'s when you speak Spanish, and that you're not speaking Spanish right now?"

Rebecca rolled her eyes before responding, "*Rrrr-r*idiculous."

* * * * * * *

For school parties, moms, and sometimes dads, sent in baked goods or, if they're really extreme, healthy snacks. But we Eights didn't have any parents around at the moment to do that for us. So while Will Simms's mom had sent in a special cooler so we could make snow cones and Mandy Stenko's father had sent in a tray of raw vegetables, we'd had to prepare something ourselves. What we brought was a case of mango juice boxes; brownies that Durinda had made, with Jackie's help; and two cans of pink frosting, one for the rest of us to put on our brownies and one for Rebecca.

"I'm going to really miss you guys over the summer," Mandy said to us, chomping on a celery stalk as we hung around the playground.

The sun felt good on our faces.

"Yeah, us too," we did our best to agree.

"I don't know what I'll do all summer without you," Will Simms said. "Maybe we could get together occasionally and find ways to get into trouble?"

Good old Will. How could we refuse?

By the time it got close to eleven thirty, and with the bouncy little yellow bus soon to arrive to transport us for the last time as third-graders, the McG, our old teacher who was now our principal, showed up with her long nose.

"So. Eights." She paused.

We waited.

"Next year. Fourth grade." She paused again.

We waited again.

"Nice job this year."

We smiled.

"But I'll be keeping my eye on you next year. Both eyes. Both eyes, a microscope, and a magnifying glass."

We frowned.

But then . . .

Beep-beep!

The bus.

Yippee! Time for summer vacation!

* * * * * * * *

That night, when seven of us crawled into bed and Petal crawled back under it, we were both shocked and pleased that we'd survived Friday the thirteenth with nothing terrible happening to us.

Petal was particularly pleased that there had been no visits from the ax murderer.

"It doesn't really mean anything," Rebecca shouted loudly enough from her bed that both bedrooms of Eights could hear her.

We waited for her to make her point.

"On New Year's Eve," she went on, "when the rest

of the world was celebrating and blowing party horns and wearing funny hats, our parents disappeared. Or died. Then on Friday the thirteenth, what do we get? Something awful or a visit from Petal's ax murderer? No, we get cans of pink frosting." She yawned. "Probably on our birthday, instead of us having a cake, the world will come to an end."

Oh, thanks, *Rrrr*rebecca. Thanks a lot!

FIVE

But the next day, Saturday, we didn't have time to think about dire things like the world coming to an end.

It was summer vacation and we were too busy getting ready for our trip—to France!

"We need to pack," Annie announced.

"But the Mr. McG said we were supposed to laze in a hammock," Georgia objected, her face falling. She'd just dragged the hammock out.

"Too bad," Annie said. "You and Rebecca, get the suitcases out of the attic. Durinda and Jackie, dust the suitcases. Marcia and Zinnia, pack suitable clothes for all of us; we'll need fancy dresses for the wedding and something comfortable for the plane . . . and don't forget the underwear! Petal, enjoy your morning under the bed."

Georgia crossed her arms over her chest and narrowed her eyes at Annie. "And what will *you* be doing while we're doing all the work?"

"I'll be driving over to Pete's Repairs and Auto Wrecking," she said with a toss of the head. "I need to see if he's got those passports yet."

* * * * * * * *

"We look like . . . criminals," Durinda said, puzzled, when Annie returned an hour later with our brand-new fake passports.

Annie shrugged. "Pete says they always come out like that, even the legal ones."

"I look like I could *rrrrr*ob a bank," Rebecca said, pleased. "Maybe when I'm in F*rrrrr*ance, I'll *rrrrr*ob the *Rrrrr*ight Bank."

Rebecca had been reading up on France, but apparently she'd missed a page.

"Right Bank refers to a side of the river," Marcia pointed out. "So you can't get money there unless you *rrrrr*ob actual people." Then she realized what she'd just said. "Oh, blast! Now you've got me doing it!"

"Oh, look!" Zinnia said. "Pete's man who knows a man who knows a man, or whatever, also put little stamps in our passports so it looks as though we've traveled all over the world. I like the idea of being a world traveler!"

"I don't like my picture," Petal, who'd come out from

under the bed long enough to see her passport, said. "I'm getting scared just looking at me."

"What about Pete's and Mrs. Pete's passports?" Jackie asked Annie. "Do they look like criminals in theirs too?"

"I don't know." Annie shrugged. "I didn't see theirs. Maybe they already had theirs and didn't need fake ones?"

* * * * * * * *

But one thing Annie did decide we all needed before our trip was haircuts.

"Oh no!" Georgia cried. "You're not getting *me* in that . . . *insane* room!"

That insane room she was referring to was the Haircutting Room. It was one of Mommy's inventions. It used to be, before a new semester started at school, we'd all go to the Haircutting Room to get our hair trimmed in our favored styles. In the Haircutting Room, scissors flew around a person's head like crazy, snipping so fast and furiously that there was always the fear that one would lose an ear or get stabbed in the eye. Since our parents' disappearance, the only one brave enough to go in there regularly had been Annie, with the exception of Jackie, who'd gone as an April Fool's joke.

We missed our parents terribly, but one nice thing about their disappearance was that none of us had to go into that shudder-making room anymore unless she really wanted to.

But now . . .

"Just look at yourselves!" Annie shouted.

"What's wrong with the way we look?" seven Eights shouted back at her.

"Go look in the mirror," Annie said with a darkness worthy of Rebecca, "and you'll see what I mean."

We went. We looked. We saw.

"Yikes!" seven Eights shouted at our reflections. "How did *that* happen?"

Somehow, miraculously, even without benefit of the services of the Haircutting Room, we'd all managed to look exactly the same since New Year's Eve, except for Jackie, who'd changed her look voluntarily.

But now?

It was as though our hair had made up for lost time overnight. Each of us had hair that was five inches longer than it had been, except for Jackie, whose hair had only grown two and a half inches since April 1, and Annie, who had hers trimmed every month. Georgia's intensely wavy hair no longer grazed her shoulders but instead cascaded almost to the middle of her back,

while Zinnia's hair was so long it trailed behind her on the floor, like a weird bridal veil.

We looked so different. We looked nothing like ourselves.

"See what I mean?" Annie said. "It's as though overnight you've all turned into those dolls whose hair keeps coming out of their fake little heads when you tug on it."

"I don't like not looking like me." Petal's lower lip began to tremble. "It's as bad as seeing myself looking evil in that passport photo."

"I have to confess, I don't like it either," Marcia said. "My bangs are down to my chin. It's like looking at the world through a hair curtain."

"What do we do about this fresh horror?" Georgia said.

Almost immediately, she regretted her question. We all did. For, instead of answering, Annie simply jerked her thumb hard to the left.

Toward the Haircutting Room.

* * * * * * * *

"Ouch!"

"Watch it!"

"Be ca*rrrrr*eful with those!"

"Cut hers next!"

"Cut me last!"

"Not me—remember, I was already in here once this month?"

"Ooh, I like that!"

"I don't like thisssssssss!"

And then it was done, another hurdle gotten over before our trip, and we were back to looking like ourselves again.

* * * * * * * *

But there were yet more hurdles.

Sunday morning, Zinnia came up with a problem. A big problem.

A *feline* problem.

"We're leaving tomorrow, June sixteenth," she said to Annie, "the wedding is on the twenty-first, and the tickets you ordered say we're due to fly back on June twenty-third, so we'll be gone for seven days. What are we going to do with our eight furry friends while we're gone?"

"We left them here by themselves when we went on vacation with Mommy and Daddy last Christmas," Annie said. "That worked out okay."

"You call it okay," Durinda asked, "coming home to find kibble in every room and half the furniture knocked over?"

"They did trash the place," Marcia said.

"No," Rebecca corrected her, eyes gleaming. "They had a party."

"Whatever you want to call it," Zinnia said, "they do it because they get lonely without us. Also because they get offended that we would leave them for so long."

"So what do you want me to do about it?" Annie sighed.

"You could call Pete and ask him what to do," Jackie said helpfully.

"You like calling Pete, Annie," Georgia said. "It makes you feel important."

"And he likes being called," Petal said.

We trooped after Annie as she went to use the phone in Mommy's private study, the only one in the house with speakerphone.

"Pete's Repairs and Auto Wrecking," we heard Pete's happy voice say a minute later. "Pete speaking."

"Annie Huit," Annie said, adding our last name as though he might not know which Annie it was otherwise. "We don't know what to do about the cats."

"Can't you leave them with a relative?" he asked, then answered himself before anyone else had the chance to. "No, of course not. All your relatives are either missing or crazy or in France. How about leaving them home alone then?" Again he answered himself. "No, that won't work. I can do that with Old Felix because he's, well, old. But what works with my one old cat would never work with your eight powerful ones. They'd trash the place."

As well we knew.

"An animal hotel, then?" he suggested.

"I really and truly don't mean to be rude, Mr. Pete," Zinnia said, "but bite your tongue. Do you not realize how abandoned that would make them feel? It would be awful for them."

"Yes, yes, what was I thinking?" Pete sounded as

though he felt terrible about what he'd said. Then he laughed. "Well, clearly I *wasn't* thinking." And now he sounded excited. "I know! Why don't we just take them on the plane?"

Cats on a plane?

Could our mechanic really be serious?

"But wouldn't we need special permission for that?" Annie said aloud what all of us were thinking. "Surely the airline must have rules . . ."

"Don't worry about it, lamb. I know a man who knows a man who . . ."

And just like that, we had one less problem to worry about.

Our eight cats were going with us—to France!

* * * * * * * *

Monday finally arrived, the day we were to depart.

We were packed. We had our fake passports. We looked spiffy.

There was just one final problem.

"We need a dozen eggs."

That was Carl the talking refrigerator, and he couldn't stop talking to us as we raced around the house grabbing last-minute items. And what he couldn't stop talking about was eggs!

"Maybe brown eggs," Carl went on, "because, well, they last longer than white eggs. But then again, white eggs tend to be easier to break, and anyhow with eight of you, neither last that long, so I don't know. Maybe we should think about a carton of Egg Beaters—you know, the stuff you pour? Doesn't that sound easier than breaking eggs and having to worry about eggshells? But do Egg Beaters cost more? I'm not sure about that. At what point does convenience outweigh cost? I don't know. Some people think Egg Beaters are healthier than regular eggs, lower cholesterol and all that—"

"Shut up!" Rebecca shouted at Carl.

"Don't yell at him!" Durinda yelled at Rebecca. "You know how sensitive he is!"

"Oh," Rebecca said, hands on hips, "like I'm not?"

We all ignored that.

"What's wrong, Carl?" Durinda patted him on the back.

Carl hadn't seemed this crazy since February when he'd started melting because he'd fallen in love with robot Betty and she hadn't realized yet that she loved him back.

"But could you make it quick, Carl?" Durinda added gently as Zinnia began rounding up all the cats. "We do have a plane to catch."

"That's the whole problem," Carl said. "It's like the

kids are all leaving the nest and I'm a parent being left behind. I don't know what to do with myself if I have no one to care for."

"Aw, that's so sweet," Rebecca said. Then she snapped, "Now can we hurry this up?"

"You're all leaving me and now Rebecca's snapping at me!" Carl yelled in anguish. Then we heard a clinking sound and saw that Carl had begun crying ice cubes.

Poor Carl.

"But you'll have robot Betty here with you," Durinda pointed out, patting Carl some more.

"Yes," Carl said. "I suppose now we will be empty nesters together. Maybe we will grow closer."

"There's the spirit!" Jackie said.

"Maybe robot Betty will fall for me all over again," Carl said. "It will be like our love is new."

We looked over at robot Betty. Even though Carl was the cooling machine, she always struck us as the colder of the two, and we worried their second honeymoon might not be all he dreamed.

Still . . .

"We really do have to go now, I'm afraid," Durinda said as we heard Pete beep his horn and realized the Petes had arrived to take us to the airport. Of course they'd come in to help us with our bags, but we liked it that they beeped first to let us know they were there. Beeps could be such cheering things.

"Just don't talk to robot Betty all the time about eggs," Georgia advised, "and you should be fine."

"We'll see you just one week from today!" we all shouted back to him as we headed for the door. We stopped to lay kisses on the foreheads of Daddy Sparky and Mommy Sally, and then we left, locking the house behind us.

Then eight girls, eight cats, one large present, and eight suitcases piled into the vehicle with the Petes, and we were on our way.

Pete had brought the limo this time, so we were going in style.

SIX

And then we were finally at the airport.

It seemed to us that it had taken forever to get there, and by that we didn't just mean the ride in the limo. We meant first deciding not to go to France; then deciding to go; then dithering about a present, passports, packing, haircuts, sad talking refrigerators, and cats. We didn't think adults would dither so much before a trip.

But then we cut ourselves some slack.

Adults go on trips all the time with no dithering. Or maybe they do dither a bit, although probably not as much as we had. But here's the thing: they *are* adults. Things are easier for them. And even though we had the Petes to accompany us, essentially we were still eight little girls who had planned a trip to a foreign country successfully and were now waiting with our tickets and fake passports to board a plane.

By our lights, when we thought about it like that, dithering and all, we hadn't done half bad!

* * * * * * * *

"Oh, I hope we don't get arrested, I hope we don't get arrested, I hope we don't get arrested," Petal kept muttering to herself as we approached our turn with the ticket taker.

"Please stop muttering like that," Annie whispered. "You're drawing more attention to us, and we're doing that well enough just fine on our own, what with Zinnia insisting we bring the cats."

Each of us held a suitcase on one side and a cat on the other.

We were taking turns balancing the present for Aunt Martha and Uncle George on our heads. It made us feel very exotic, like African villagers, but it was heavy.

"I can't help it," Petal said. "I don't want to go to jail for having a fake passport. I'd scare myself in the mirror if I had to wear black-and-white stripes and a cap to match."

"Don't worry." Rebecca sneered. "They wear orange jumpsuits instead now."

"That's not helpful," Annie reprimanded Rebecca.

But when it came our turn, the ticket taker simply

looked over all our fake passports, the ones in which we looked like hardened criminals, without a change in her calm expression.

What did change the calm of her expression was the sight of each of us holding a cat.

"You can't bring those on the plane like that, I'm afraid," she said. "They each need to be placed in a separate carrier. Did you bring eight carriers?"

Zinnia looked about to cry, but then Pete stepped up and spoke to the ticket taker in a hushed tone.

"It's all right, luv," he said. "You see, I know a man who knows a man who—"

And then we heard him whisper the name of one of the men.

It was a name we'd all heard before. It was a very famous name.

Who knew Pete the mechanic was *so* well connected?

"Well, in that case . . ." The ticket taker blushed. "Oh! I almost forgot! Can I see your passport?"

Pete handed his over and handed Mrs. Pete's over as well.

Eight heads peered around the side of the ticket taker so we could see if the Petes' passport photos were as hideous as ours.

Funny thing, that. They looked completely normal and nice in their photos, exactly like themselves. But hang on. That last name . . .

"Thank you, Mr. Zero." The ticket taker smiled as she handed the Petes' passports back to them. "Mrs. Zero."

We waited to react until we were far enough away from the ticket taker but not too close to the pilot who stood at the door of the airplane, because even we knew it would look suspicious if we were surprised about the last name of the adults we were traveling with.

"Zero?" we whisper-shouted. "Your last name's Zero, making you Pete Zero and Jill Zero?"

"I know," Pete said with a sorry shrug. "And now you know why I prefer to be known simply as Pete."

* * * * * * * *

Eights on a plane!

Two years ago there had been a horror movie out in the theaters. It was called *Snakes on a Plane.* We wanted to see it, even though we were only five years old at the time. Well, Rebecca wanted to go, bad. And Georgia said she wanted to go too, but we suspected that was just to impress Rebecca. Zinnia worried that the snakes had been mistreated by the moviemakers, and Petal wanted no part of any of it.

We did get to see advertisements for it on TV. It was Mommy who said we couldn't go. She said it would be too scary, and she had to keep reminding Rebecca that she was only five, so even if Rebecca did break into her own piggy bank, take all her pennies, and walk the six miles to the movie theater, they wouldn't let her in by herself. Mommy actually did sound sorry to have to disappoint Rebecca—she always hated to disappoint any of us—but she still wasn't about to say yes.

It was Daddy, though, who said those advertisements were the most amazing thing he'd ever seen. He referred to them as "high concept."

When we'd asked him what that meant—we didn't think to ask Jackie because she had yet to swallow a dictionary—he explained that *high concept* meant that you could immediately grasp the whole idea of a movie or a book just from one sentence.

"And here they've done it all in just the title!" he'd gone on, still amazed. "They don't even have to run those full commercials with the snakes falling from the ceiling, because it's all, everything, right there in the title: *Snakes on a Plane!* What could be more obvious?"

"Kind of like frosting-covered hot dogs on a stick, right, Daddy?" Rebecca had said. "You know exactly what wonderful thing you're getting just from the name."

We'd ignored Rebecca when she'd said that—so gross. Right now we were living our own high-concept life, so let us say it again: *Eights on a plane!*

We think people will get the picture.

* * * * * * * *

But just to fill in a few of the details . . .

We were chaos.

It took us forever to figure out which seats were ours, then to stow our luggage in the overhead bin, then to settle down with our cats.

And of course there were a few other people on the plane as well, all trying to do similar things, minus the cats.

Then the pilot's voice came over the loudspeaker and announced that we'd missed our chance to get in line to take off because we'd all taken too long to settle in, so there would be a slight delay in our departure.

Rebecca and Georgia took this as an invitation to play catch in the aisle with Rambunctious, which horrified many people, including Zinnia, but which Petal didn't notice because she was hiding under her seat.

Thankfully, the cat did not seem to mind being treated as a sporting good.

But the flight attendant did mind, so he hurried them back to their seats, dragged Petal out from under hers, and offered us all complimentary beverages.

"Coffee for me, please," Annie said.

"I would like some juice," Marcia said.

"Do you have any mango juice?" Jackie asked.

We were seated in rows of two as follows, from front to back: The Petes; Annie and Durinda; Georgia and Jackie; Marcia and Petal; Rebecca and Zinnia.

Now that we thought about it, we wondered why it had taken us so long to figure out where we were supposed to sit, and yet it had.

"Do you think they'll show a movie?" Jackie asked.

"I hope they show *Snakes on a Plane*." Rebecca's eyes gleamed.

"Don't be nutty," Marcia said, which was a rather harsh thing to hear from her. "No reputable airline is going to show *Snakes on a Plane* on a plane!"

We had our coffee and juice, then the flight attendant cleared the cups away, and the pilot announced it was finally time for takeoff.

We were so excited by now, we really were bouncing in our seats.

It was almost too good to believe. It felt like we were going on our greatest adventure ever!

"Are we there yet, Mr. Pete?" Georgia called forward before we'd even left the ground.

"Not yet," he replied patiently.

Then we were taxiing down the runway; the sun was setting, and we could feel our bodies in the plane slowly leaving the earth, climbing higher at a steady angle.

It was all so amazing! So aerodynamic!

"Are we there yet, Mr. Pete?" Georgia called forward again.

"Not for a while," he said. "At least another hour, maybe seven."

"Perhaps you Eights should try to get some rest," Mrs. Pete suggested. "There is a time difference. You don't want to get jet lag, and a nap might help to confuse your bodies."

Ooh! Jet lag! We hadn't thought of that.

And we did so want to be fresh when we arrived at our destination, where we'd be seeing old relatives, perhaps meeting new ones, celebrating matrimony, and eating cake. Plus, we'd have to be on our best behavior and be polite the whole time, which we well knew could be exhausting work.

So we heeded Mrs. Pete's advice.

We pulled the little plastic shutters over our little airplane windows and turned off the little round reading lights overhead. Then we asked the flight attendant to get our little pillows from the overhead bins, and although we were tempted by the movie they were showing on the flight—which was *not,* we feel the need to point out, *Snakes on a Plane*—we shut our eyes and thought sweet thoughts until we fell asleep.

Well, maybe Rebecca didn't think sweet thoughts— who knew with her?—but the rest of us didn't like to think too much about that.

It seemed like our heads had only just touched the pillows (though later on we would learn that it had in fact been a few hours since we'd fallen asleep) when the scream woke us up.

"Where are we? Where are we?" we all said, blinking around in that startled way people do when they wake in unfamiliar surroundings.

We blinked around some more and turned on the overhead reading lights and pushed up the little plastic shutters so we could see out our little airplane windows.

But it was all darkness, with nothing to see out there but the blinking red lights on the wings of the plane.

Some of us suspected that the darkness meant we were flying over an ocean. We don't know why we thought this, but it made sense to us at the time.

Then the scream came again, and we realized it was Petal screaming.

A moment later we realized that for once she had something to scream about.

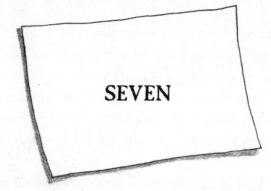

SEVEN

Pete the mechanic unbuckled his seat belt and was out of his chair and at Petal's side quicker than we had ever imagined a man with weight hanging over the top of his jeans could move.

"Petal, what's wrong?" he asked.

Then Mrs. Pete, moving quickly, was there too.

"Did you have a bad dream?" she asked, crouching down beside Petal.

"No!" Petal cried. "We're not going to France after all . . . and I'm scared!"

"I can't believe you woke us all up for this." Rebecca was cross. "Of course we're going to France. We're in a plane and that's where we're headed."

"No, we're not," Petal said. "I heard . . . *him*."

"Him?" Annie echoed.

"Who did you hear?" Durinda asked gently.

"Oh no," Georgia said. "Petal's starting to hear voices. She must finally have gone completely around the bend."

"Fear can do that to a person," Marcia said wisely. "There have been scientific studies."

"I hope her cat doesn't go crazy too," Zinnia said. "Being crazy would be very hard on poor Precious."

"I didn't hear voices in my head," Petal said, sounding impatient with us. "I heard that man. The man behind the door."

She pointed, and we all followed her finger toward the front of the plane.

"That's the cockpit," Jackie said. "Do you mean the pilot?"

"Yes." Petal nodded fearfully. "Yes, that's it."

"But that's impossible," Pete said. "That door is steel and it's very thick."

"I don't think you could have heard him talking through that, dear," Mrs. Pete said gently. Then her eyes brightened, as though she'd just gotten a good idea. "Did he maybe speak over the intercom? And perhaps the rest of us didn't hear because we were so sound asleep?"

"No!" It was very rare for Petal to be so impatient, particularly with an adult, but she was now. "I didn't hear him talking to someone else. And I didn't hear him over the intercom." She paused, then went on, sounding terrified yet insistent. *"I heard the voice in his head!"*

In most families, if one of their members started talking about hearing voices in other people's heads, that person would probably get locked away somewhere.

But we weren't like most families, never had been, and even Georgia, who'd talked about Petal finally going around the bend, could see that such a thing might be significant.

"What was his voice saying?" Pete asked urgently.

"It said, 'I'm changing direction on this plane.'" Petal paused. "He spoke with a funny accent, although I guess sometimes we do too, but I couldn't place his. And then he said, 'I need to get back to Italia, *pronto.*'"

"What does that mean?" Rebecca asked. "*Italia* and *pronto*? I only speak Spanish, you see."

"You speak English too," Georgia said. "In fact, you're doing that now."

"It means 'Italy' and 'fast,'" Pete said, straightening up. "It also means I need to get to the bottom of this."

He strode manfully toward the front of the cabin.

"Oh no!" Petal cried. "I can't go to Italy! I've only just recently wrapped my mind around going to France. If I have to wrap my mind around a different country now, I'll go crazy!"

"I think you already are," Rebecca said.

"That's not helpful," Annie said sharply to Rebecca.

Now Pete was pounding on the cockpit door, and the flight attendant was rushing over to him.

"You can't go in there, sir," he said, trying to restrain Pete.

"You think that, do you?" Pete said mildly. "Well, watch me."

Then Pete proceeded to pound on the door some more, shouting, "Oh, Captain! My captain! You'd better get out here and explain yourself!"

"Please get back in your seat, sir!" the flight attendant ordered Pete, to no avail.

Pete kept pounding and yelling, "Oh, Captain! My captain!" and a moment later, the cockpit door flew open.

The pilot stood there in the doorway, hair wild and tie loose.

"How may I help you, *signore*?"

Petal was right. He did have a funny accent. Until that moment, we'd still been thinking that there was a good chance Petal was wrong and that maybe she really was crazy.

But hang on.

Petal could hear the voices in other people's heads?

We didn't have time just then to think on what that could mean in general, or what it could mean specifically for us, because Pete had started talking rapidly to the pilot, who was talking just as rapidly back, making wild gestures with his hands all the while.

There was just one problem.

We couldn't understand a word they were saying.

"What language is that?" Annie wondered.

"I don't know," Marcia said. "Maybe Italian? That would make sense since they do both keep saying *Italia*."

We were stunned.

Pete was bilingual?

"Pete's bilingual?" Jackie said aloud.

"Oh yes," Mrs. Pete said proudly. "In fact, he's decalingual. He can speak ten languages, and just last week he said he wanted to start on Chinese."

Huh.

Who knew?

In his own way, Pete was definitely a man of mystery.

And now he was doing something really mysterious. He was accepting rope from the flight attendant—we hadn't heard him ask for rope, but maybe he'd asked in Italian?—and using it to tie the pilot's hands behind his back.

What was going on here?

The other passengers—and there *were* other passengers on that plane with us, although we kept forgetting all about them—had so far taken everything that had happened in stride. But something about seeing the pilot with his hands tied behind his back proved too much for them.

Come to think of that, it proved too much for us too.

"Who's flying the plane?" Petal shrieked in a panic.

Pete ignored that as he addressed the cabin.

"I'm sorry, folks, but there will be a brief delay in our arriving to France. You see, the pilot here thought he'd make a slight detour . . . to Italy."

"I only wanted to visit my *mamma*," the pilot said sadly.

"You mean we were being hijacked?" Rebecca said. Then she turned and punched Petal in the shoulder. "Why didn't you say something about hearing voices sooner?"

"I think *hijacked* is too harsh a word," Pete said.

"More like a detour. Poor Guido here simply wanted to visit his *mamma*."

"*Sì,*" Pilot Guido said. "It is her birthday, and the airline wouldn't give me any time off."

"Aw." The entire plane heaved a sympathetic sigh. Who couldn't understand someone wanting to see his mother so much on her birthday that he'd be willing to resort to superhuman efforts to get there?

We could certainly understand that. We'd been without a mother for nearly six months now, and we'd love to see her on her birthday. We'd love to see her again any day.

"Yes, I know," Pete agreed. "It is very sad that Pilot Guido can't be with his *mamma* on her birthday, but surely you can see now why he must be restrained for the time being and why he can't be trusted to fly the plane, at least not tonight."

Petal raised her hand timidly, as though we were in class back at the Whistle Stop.

"Excuse me? Mr. Pete?" she called out softly when he failed to notice her increasingly wildly waving hand.

"Yes, Petal?"

"If the pilot's out here and he's, er, all tied up . . ." Petal paused, gestured to the open cockpit door. "Then who's flying the plane? Come to think of it, who's *been* flying the plane since you dragged Pilot Guido out here? Because, you see, I've been trying very hard to concentrate, and I don't hear any voices coming from in there, not a single one at all, so—"

"Oh! Right!" Pete said, thrusting the bound pilot in the general direction of the flight attendant. "I knew I was forgetting something."

Then Pete rushed into the cockpit, the door flapping but remaining open behind him.

We all craned our necks into the aisle so we could see what was going on, and what we saw was Pete assuming the pilot's seat and fiddling with the control panel of the plane.

"What's he doing?" Zinnia asked in a hushed voice.

Georgia's eyes were round as saucers. "I think he's going to fly the plane!"

Eight heads swiveled in Mrs. Pete's direction.

"Can he do that?" Annie demanded. "Does he know how to fly a plane?"

"Why not?" Mrs. Pete said. "After all, you learned how to drive a car."

"Yes, I know," Annie said, "but I do think flying a plane might be a bit more complicated than that."

Mrs. Pete shrugged. "He read a book on it once, I think. He'll figure it out. He has to."

"Don't they usually have copilots on these things?" Marcia wondered. "I'm sure they do."

"Must be a low-budget operation," Rebecca said darkly.

Before we could think further on this, Pilot Pete spoke to us over the intercom.

"Ladies and gentlemen," he said. "I've readjusted our flight pattern, and we are once again on target for France."

A cry of "Yay!" went up within the cabin.

Well, except for poor Pilot Guido.

"Now, before I go back to flying the plane," Pete said, "I'd just like everyone here to know that, while I can't tell you quite how she did it, we would all be in Italy soon were it not for passenger Petal Huit. Not that there's anything generally wrong with going to Italy, but it's no good if you're supposed to be in France. So how about a big round of applause for passenger Petal."

The plane cheered and clapped.

Petal blushed.

Then we all settled back, content to let Pete do what he did best: save us.

Even Petal was peaceful for once, but it lasted for only a minute.

"Oh no!" she cried. "I got my power! But I don't want my power! Take it back! Take it back! I don't want to be able to read other people's minds!"

Some of us weren't sure we wanted her to be able to do that either.

"Oh, I think I'm going to be sick!" Petal cried. Then

she reached into the pocket on the back of the seat in front of her, probably hoping to find an airsickness bag.

But what her hand pulled out wasn't an airsickness bag at all. It was a note.

We'd seen notes like this one before, but they were usually found behind a loose stone in our drawing room back home.

With trembling hands, Petal held the note and read.

Dear Petal,

Eleven down, five to go. Try not to worry too much!

As always, the note was unsigned.

Petal fainted then, of course, leaving the rest of us to wonder:

How did the person who usually left the notes for us at home manage to get one to us on a plane?

What a magical invisible person!

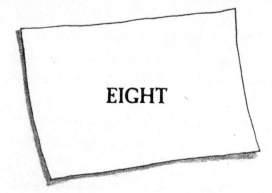

EIGHT

When the plane touched down in France, we looked out our windows and saw that morning was just dawning.

We'd left one country when the sun was setting and arrived in another one with a new day just starting. This struck us as odd, but then we just figured that maybe air travel was like that.

We also thought that it felt like it had taken forever for us to get here, but then we further figured that maybe the point of things wasn't just the destination; maybe the journey counted for something too.

Aunt Martha and Uncle George were waiting there to greet us inside the airport terminal.

We studied these relatives we hadn't seen for a very long time.

Funny, we thought. Aunt Martha, Daddy's sister, always worried that everything she wore made her look fat, and yet she wasn't fat at all—not that there'd be anything wrong with it if she were. She certainly

wasn't model thin, but she was tall and regular thin, and even pretty, with black hair and gray eyes.

As for Uncle George, now that we knew he was Mommy's brother, we could see the family resemblance. He had brown hair and eyes, just like Mommy and us, and he looked nice enough. We only hoped he wouldn't try to cook us anything.

We had to admit, we were surprised at how happy they were to see us. We didn't remember any relatives other than Mommy and Daddy loving us quite so much. Crazy Serena certainly hadn't. Why, she'd tried to Eightnap us!

"Eights!" Aunt Martha cried, pulling us all in for a hug. It was a bit of a tight squeeze for the cats, but somehow we managed. "I'm so happy you could make it!"

"Me too," Uncle George said, also embracing us. "But I'm so sorry Robert and Lucy couldn't come. Of course, as it turns out, a few other significant people couldn't come either."

Hug over, we did the polite thing and introduced them to the Petes, and then they did the polite thing in not blinking too hard when they learned the Petes' last name was Zero.

"You can just call us Pete and Jill," Pete said.

"We're so happy to be here," Mrs. Pete said. "Who ever would have thought of getting married in France?"

"I don't know," Uncle George said, looking surprised. "I suppose French people think of it all the time."

"Come along," Aunt Martha said cheerfully. "Let's get your bags. We've got a big car to take us all to the chateau. It's where the entire wedding party will be staying."

"What's a chateau?" Petal whispered. "Is it like a dungeon?"

"No," Jackie whispered. "It's a large country house or mansion in the French countryside."

That didn't sound so impressive to us. After all, we already lived in a great stone house almost as big as a mansion.

* * * * * * * *

The chateau did turn out to be very large, with turrets and some sort of river running outside all the way around, but we were hardly impressed. We did have our own tower room back home, and we doubted this place had any seasonal rooms, which always come in handy. One thing that did impress us: all of the ceilings in the rooms were *incredibly* high, whereas back home we only had one room with a ceiling like that.

"I'll just show you to your rooms," Aunt Martha said, "and then I'll leave you to unpack. And perhaps you'd like to take a nap? You must be jet-lagged, and we are having a big party tonight. In fact, we're having parties every night this week, right up till the wedding."

Talk about overdoing a thing. We hoped she didn't expect us to give her a present every night. We'd only brought the one.

"Oh, and Petal," Aunt Martha said in a chipper voice before leaving us to our own devices, "I have a special surprise for you!"

"Not a special surprise!" Petal cried. "I don't want a special surprise! Why am I being singled out? And can't you tell me what it is now? I'll get a headache if I don't know."

"Oh, you'll like this surprise," Aunt Martha said.

"And it has to be you, because you're the perfect person for the job."

"Job?" Petal cried. "You mean I have to work? I'm fairly certain there are child-labor laws against that!"

But Aunt Martha failed to hear that last part because she'd already disappeared down the long hallway.

Petal threw her little body down on the bed in misery. "Oops! Wrong position," she said, popping up again, after which she dived under the bed.

New country, new bed, same Petal.

A second later, Petal's cat, Precious, dived in after her. Now both girl and cat were cowering. Perhaps Precious had received her power and was scared of it too?

Of course she had. That's the way the world worked.

"Surely you've learned by now that this routine won't work." Annie sighed.

"Don't care" came Petal's muffled voice.

"New country, new bed, same Rebecca." Rebecca's eyes gleamed as she rolled up her sleeves.

"Hang on," Annie said, waving Rebecca away for the moment.

This was probably a mistake on Annie's part. Rebecca did *not* like to be waved away.

"Can you tell us why you're hiding under the bed this time?" Annie said. "You've already got your power, so it's not like you can avoid getting it by hiding."

"But I don't want to use it" came the muffled voice. "It's too scary. And I don't want whatever special surprise Aunt Martha has planned for me. That's scary too. I figure maybe if I stay under here forever, I won't have to deal with the special surprise, plus the muffling of the bed will keep me from reading people's minds."

"And how's that working out for you?" Georgia asked.

"Not so good," Petal admitted. "I just heard you think, 'Petal's a little idiot.'"

Georgia at least had the grace to look embarrassed at having her mind read. Rebecca smirked.

"But I'm sure I can get better at it in time," the muffled voice said forcefully, "if I just put my mind to it."

"Doesn't it take up lots of mental energy being so scared all the time?" Jackie asked in a kind way.

"It is tiring," Petal admitted. "Sometimes I exhaust myself."

"I know!" Marcia said. "Annie, why don't you make up one of those pro-and-con lists you do!"

"That's an excellent idea!" Durinda agreed. "Like that time I wasn't sure I wanted my power."

"Oh, I love it when Annie makes those lists," Zinnia said. "It's like playing a game."

"Very well," Annie said. "Where can I find a pencil and paper . . ."

She located the items in a desk drawer, which is just where a person would imagine they'd be.

"Right," Annie said. "Now, why don't we start with cons, since you're always so negative, Petal."

"Fine," Petal said, "although I don't appreciate being called negative, even if I am. Cons: One, it's scary. Two, it's scary. Three, it's scary. Four, it's—"

"We get the idea," Annie said, cutting her off.

"She does have a point, you know," Jackie said with a shrug. "If you can read people's minds, what happens when you hear something you wish you hadn't, like Georgia thinking Petal's a little idiot?"

"Ex*actly*," the muffled voice said firmly.

"But what about the pros?" Marcia said. "Think how wonderful it would be in so many ways."

"You'd know what Durinda was planning for dinner," Georgia said. "And if you didn't like it, you could persuade her to make something different. You know, if what she originally planned was awful or something."

"Hey!" Durinda was outraged. "Nothing I make is awful."

We ignored her.

"I don't care about food anymore," Petal said.

"You'd always know in advance what homework assignment the teacher was going to give," Zinnia said. Then she got really excited. "Ooh, it could be like Marcia seeing the answers on that test that time with her x-ray vision. You'd be able to read the answers straight from the teacher's mind!"

"That's cheating," Annie said firmly. "We don't cheat anymore."

"Besides," Petal said, "it's summer vacation. Who cares about school right now?"

"You could read the minds of evil people," Rebecca said, "and then once you know what they're planning, *you* can plan an evil strategy to get them before they get you."

"That's exactly the sort of thing that terrifies me," Petal said.

We were getting frustrated.

"So much for your great pro-and-con lists," Rebecca said, sneering at Annie.

"I've got an idea," Jackie said, excited. "We're your sisters, Petal. What could be less scary than reading our minds? So why don't you come out from under the bed, just for a few minutes, and try your new power on all of us. Maybe that'll make it all less frightening for you."

We all thought that was a good idea, even Rebecca. Even Petal did, shockingly enough, because she slowly slid backward out from under the bed and got up, Precious slithering backward and out beside her.

We looked at Petal standing there, hair tousled. It was nice not to be talking to her feet anymore.

"Why don't you start with me," Jackie said gently.

Petal tilted her head to one side and stared at Jackie's forehead.

We waited to see what would happen, and a moment later we were startled to see a smile break across Petal's face.

"What am I thinking?" Jackie asked.

"You're thinking, 'I love Petal and only want to help her.'" Petal smiled some more. "Gee, that's not too bad."

"Do Zinnia next," Jackie suggested.

Petal tilted her head to the side again and this time stared at Zinnia's forehead.

"Zinnia's thinking," Petal said, "'Even though I never wanted one before and don't know what I'd do with one now, I wish I could keep the Deluxe Perfect-Every-Time Hamburger Maker/Manicure-Pedicure Machine we bought as a wedding present for Aunt Martha and Uncle George.'" Petal laughed. "That's kind of funny."

"And Durinda," Jackie said.

"Durinda's thinking, 'I'll bet dinner tonight won't be nearly as good as I could make it.'"

Durinda looked ashamed at having her immodest thought exposed.

"And Annie," Jackie said.

"Annie's thinking, 'Why am I letting Jackie run the show right now? *I* always run the show!'" Petal laughed again. "That's really funny. I was just wondering also why Annie was letting Jackie take over."

"And Marcia," Annie said, seizing control once more.

"Marcia's thinking, 'That drawer that had the pencil and paper in it—I wonder if there are any math workbooks in there. I could really use some math right around now.' Why, this isn't bad at all!" Petal said. "It seems most people just think nice, ordinary things.

Maybe you're all correct. Maybe it won't be so bad having my power."

"And Georgia," Annie said.

"Georgia's thinking . . . oh." Petal's face fell. "Georgia's still thinking, 'Petal's a little idiot.'"

"Don't mind Georgia," Jackie said.

"Yeah," Georgia said, "don't mind me. You know how I am. I get something in my head and it just sticks there for a long time, like it's attached to my brain by a piece of gum."

"And Rebecca," Annie said.

Petal tilted her head to the side one last time and stared at Rebecca's forehead.

Then she shrieked and dived back under the bed.

Precious, who'd been keeping pace with Petal, did the same thing with Rambunctious: tilted, stared, meowed loudly, dived.

"What did you read in Rebecca's mind?" six of us who weren't under the bed asked. The seventh didn't ask because they were her thoughts; she already knew them.

"It was so dark in there," Petal said, her voice trembling. "I could see almost nothing, no real words, just this vast darkness . . . and cobwebs . . . and a few spiders . . ."

Most people would be embarrassed to have the contents of their minds exposed in the way that Rebecca's had just been, and yet Rebecca looked rather proud of herself.

Poor Petal, though. Most of us were beginning to see why this power would be terrifying for her.

"And that's it?" Jackie said gently. "Nothing else but the darkness and the other nasty things you described?"

"Well," Petal admitted, "right in the center of it all, there was a giant can of pink frosting."

At least that was something.

* * * * * * * *

It took all the powers of persuasion we had to get Petal to come out from under the bed that night so we could all make an appearance at the first party for Aunt Martha and Uncle George.

When we did finally get downstairs, we were greeted by a large roomful of people, none of whom we recognized, save for Aunt Martha and Uncle George and the Petes.

Then we saw someone who looked vaguely familiar from behind, something about her hair, which was long, the color of chestnuts.

She was standing in front of the unlit fireplace,

and when she turned we could see that she had eyes the color of chocolate and was tall, like Mommy, and beautiful, like Mommy, and about ten years younger than Mommy.

We knew that woman.

Crazy Serena.

NINE

"What's she doing here?" seven Eights hissed.

To which Petal added, "I feel faint!"

"Read her mind, Petal," Annie directed. "Tell us what she's thinking so we know what she's up to."

But Petal didn't tilt her head to one side as we'd seen her do when reading our minds. Rather, she squinched her eyes shut and began mumbling nonsense words, stringing them all together so it came out sounding something like *sgfeuogfgevcsgel*. Nonstop.

She didn't tell us what she was doing—she couldn't, because she was too busy babbling nonsense—but we guessed she was doing it to drown out all sounds from other people's minds so that she couldn't hear whatever dark and terrifying thoughts lurked in Crazy Serena's.

In a way, we could understand her fear—who, except for maybe Rebecca, would want to travel into the heart of darkness?—but it was *so* not helpful.

So while Petal continued babbling with her eyes squinched shut, we dragged her over to where Aunt Martha and Uncle George stood talking to some guests.

"What's she doing here?" we asked Aunt Martha, not hissing the words this time and keeping our voices as calm as we could as we pointed to Crazy Serena.

But it wasn't Aunt Martha who answered. It was Uncle George.

"You mean my sister?" he said, looking surprised. "Also your mother's sister?"

Oh no. This was a terrible moment in our lives. Ever since we'd learned that Serena's real last name was Smith, just like Mommy's before she got married, and ever since we'd seen that picture on Mommy's computer of Mommy with Crazy Serena and a woman who looked almost exactly like Mommy, we'd kind of known that Crazy Serena was some sort of relative. If we'd thought about it more carefully, we would have realized sooner that Crazy Serena was Mommy's younger sister. But that's the thing: we hadn't *wanted* to look at it more carefully, because then we'd have had to admit to ourselves that Crazy Serena was a much closer relative than we were comfortable with her being.

But now we had to admit it. We had no choice.

Crazy Serena was our aunt.

Did that mean we had to start calling her *Aunt* Crazy Serena?

We shuddered at the thought.

"Oh, that's right," Uncle George said, his puzzled expression clearing. "You've never met her because she and your mother haven't exactly been close the last several years."

Not close? That was rich. Aunt Crazy Serena had tried to Eightnap her own sister's children. Mommy may not have known about this, wherever she was, but we knew that if she had known, she would not have been pleased.

"Would you like me to introduce you?" Uncle George offered kindly.

"To whom?" Annie asked, only half listening.

We couldn't blame her for that half-listening thing. We were distracted too. How could we not be when we'd just bumped into one of our greatest enemies in France and then immediately learned she was closely related?

"Why, to your Aunt Serena, of course," Uncle George said.

"I'd rather eat nails," Georgia blurted out.

"Pardon?" Uncle George blinked.

"What she *meant* to say," Annie said, "was, 'Do you have any snails?' We've heard they eat them in France."

"Oh yes. Yes, of course," Aunt Martha said. "Let me show you."

We found the food table and did not eat the snails.

Instead, we grabbed a few of whatever nonsnail items we could find and then circulated through the room, which is what you do at parties.

The only problem was, all the other guests were adults, so as we circulated we felt like we were snaking around trees in a redwood forest. This was particularly awkward for Petal. We tried to remember to lead her through neatly, but with her eyes squinched shut so, whenever we forgot to lead her she'd crash into people.

That was bad enough, but what was worse was that Petal was drawing even more attention to us with her incessant babbling. People were looking at us as though we had a crazy person in the family. Of course, we *did* have a crazy person in the family, several of them, but Petal was far from the worst of our crazies.

We looked at the worst of our crazies, Mommy's sister, long and hard. And then we looked around the room and saw Pete staring at her too. The last time he'd seen her, he'd kicked her out of our town. We could imagine what a satisfying moment that must have been for him, but he seemed troubled now. We could understand that. He no doubt wanted to know what was going on in Crazy Serena's mind, as did we all.

Of course Petal could have helped us out with that, but it had become increasingly obvious *that* wasn't going to happen.

We edged closer to Crazy Serena, where she now stood talking to Aunt Martha and Uncle George.

"It's such a shame Queen and her family couldn't be here," Crazy Serena was saying. "She always did love a good party so. And to miss your wedding?"

"What's she talking about?" Annie muttered low enough so as not to be heard by the adults but nowhere near loud enough to drown out Petal's babbling, which now drew Crazy Serena's stare.

"She really must be loony," Durinda said.

"She thinks she knows the queen," Georgia said.

"I hate to say it," Jackie said, "but only really crazy people think things like that."

"Maybe she does know the queen," Marcia observed. "I mean, why would she say it if she doesn't?"

"I don't think she knows the queen at all," Zinnia said. "If she did, she'd have mentioned it around us sooner. It's the sort of thing people boast about. I know I would."

"Tguewigfauifvuiawg," said Petal.

Curiously enough, Rebecca said nothing. For once, she was simply observing.

We began to worry that now that Crazy Serena was revealed to be a relative for sure, Rebecca would adopt her as a role model.

Crazy Serena tore her stare away from Petal and

turned her attention back to Aunt Martha and Uncle George.

"Yes, it is such a shame Queen and her brood couldn't be here," she said, adding, "but then Lucy's not here either, is she?"

She was referring to our mother. We resented that.

We also couldn't understand what Mommy had to do with the queen.

"Yes," Uncle George said sadly, "it is all such a shame. And so odd, Queen calling at the last minute to say she wasn't going to be able to make it. I wonder what she had to do that was so important?"

He seemed to get over his sadness very quickly, though, because his eyes lit up as he saw someone across the room.

"Oh, look!" he said to Aunt Martha. "There's my second cousin Mitch Smith—let's go say hello."

He took Aunt Martha's elbow and led her away.

We all looked at one another. What kind of name was Mitch Smith? It didn't exactly roll off the tongue, did it?

Crazy Serena glared over at us.

Seven pairs of eyes plus one squinched pair glared right back.

"Oh, this is *rrrrr*idiculous," Rebecca announced, going all Spanish on us again. "I'll just go over there and talk to the woman, find out what she's up to this time. I

mean, yes, she was obviously invited here, but she must be up to something else."

We should have stopped her, we realized that later, but it was such a shock seeing Rebecca take positive action about anything that we were dumbstruck.

We watched as Rebecca grabbed Crazy Serena's elbow, far less gently than Uncle George had taken Aunt Martha's.

Crazy Serena looked surprised by the frontal attack.

"Who are you?" Rebecca demanded. "I mean, we know who you are. Now. But what have you done with Mommy?"

"I don't know what you're talking about, you silly child." Crazy Serena yanked her arm away. "I only *wish* I knew where your mother was hiding herself these days."

"I'll bet," Rebecca said. "Now answer my questions. On Mommy's computer we saw—"

But we never got to hear her finish asking her first question, because Crazy Serena began backing away from Rebecca, slowly at first and then snaking more quickly through the crowd, with Rebecca hurrying after her, so all we could hear were little snippets from Rebecca: "Frank Freud . . . the Wicket . . ." While from Crazy Serena all we could hear was the same thing over and over: "Get away from me, you wretched child."

Other guests just chose to ignore them, but it certainly caught Pete's attention. We didn't need to hear everything Rebecca and Crazy Serena said, however, because we could guess: Rebecca wanted Crazy Serena to explain what Crazy Serena's picture was doing in a file on Mommy's computer that also contained pictures of Frank Freud and the Wicket, two of our other enemies, while Crazy Serena kept accusing Rebecca of being a wretched child.

We didn't need to be mind readers to figure that out.

But we would have had to be mind readers to guess what Aunt Martha had on her mind when she interrupted our observation of Rebecca and Crazy Serena's bizarre little dance through the crowd.

"Excuse me, Petal?" Aunt Martha asked. "Can I speak to you about that special surprise now?"

"Dreaoiiwjfeah," said Petal.

Since Rebecca was too occupied elsewhere to provide the desperate measures that were called for in these desperate times, Annie did the job all by herself.

She used one hand to force open one of Petal's eyes so she could see Aunt Martha, even if it was in monovision, while she used the other hand to clamp Petal's mouth shut so that there'd be no more babbling.

"Go ahead." Annie nodded at Aunt Martha. "But make it quick. I'm not sure how long I can hold her like this."

"Petal?" Aunt Martha said. "I'm sure all the girls would like to have the honor, because it's the sort of thing all little girls dream of doing, but I singled you out because you have the perfect name for the job. It's as though you were born for it." Aunt Martha paused. "Would you be my flower girl?"

Aunt Martha was right about one thing, proving she was that rare family member who might just have a head on her shoulders. Yes, being asked to be a flower girl was what most little girls dreamed of doing.

There was just one problem. Petal Huit had never been a member of "most little girls." Come to think of it, none of us had.

So Petal did the Petal Huit thing to do, given the situation.

She shrieked, *"No!"* in horror.

Then she fainted.

Then when she woke from fainting, she raced upstairs and dived under the bed.

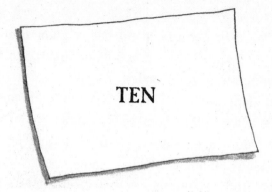

TEN

Once again we were all crouched around the bottom of a bed trying to talk some sense into Petal, only this time Aunt Martha was there with us. Turned out we were the kind of kids who could drag another relative down with them like nobody's business.

"It's so difficult to have a conversation with you like this," Annie said.

"Talk to the feet" came the muffled voice.

"But I don't understand, dear." Aunt Martha was clearly puzzled. "What sort of girl doesn't want to be a flower girl?"

"Me" came the muffled answer.

"But I still don't understand," Aunt Martha said.

"Because it scares me," Petal said. "And anyway, why can't Zinnia do it? She loves doing that sort of thing. And she's got the perfect name for it too, since obviously you're just looking for a girl whose name has something to do with a flower."

For once in her life, Petal had a point there; two, actually. Zinnia *did* love that sort of thing, and she *did* have the name of a flower.

"But don't you see?" Aunt Martha said, preparing to shoot down Petal's points. "Your name is even more perfect. Petal. Ever since I heard you were coming to the wedding after all, I thought how cute it would be, someone whose name was actually Petal strewing rose petals from a basket all down the aisle."

Aunt Martha was determined. We were fast learning there was little point in trying to get between a bride and what she wants.

But then, Aunt Martha had never come up against Petal, or at least she hadn't seen Petal in a very long while.

"But that's the whole terrifying part," Petal said. "Me? Petal? Strewing petals down an aisle for other people to walk on? It would be like ripping off little pieces of myself and throwing them away. Surely, even if you are the bride, you can't expect me to do *that*."

And another point for Petal, because when she put it like that . . .

"I guess I hadn't thought—" Aunt Martha started to say, but Petal cut her off.

"No, clearly you hadn't. But that's the thing: people hardly ever think when it comes to me. I'm sorry to spoil your plans for your big day, but nope, sorry, can't help you out here, try someone else, please call again when it's all over with."

"Well, seeing as you feel so strongly about it . . ." Aunt Martha rose to her feet. "Zinnia, can you help me out? I do still need a flower girl."

"Gladly." Zinnia's smile was as wide as a river. "I don't even care if you want me to carry zinnias and rip them to shreds."

We knew Zinnia would react that way to such an offer.

"Well, I don't think we need to go that far," Aunt Martha said, "but thank you."

Then she was gone.

And so ended Monday, our first day in France.

* * * * * * * *

We spent the remainder of the week leading up to the wedding sightseeing in the daytime and going to parties in the chateau at night.

On Tuesday we saw the Right Bank and the Left Bank.

On Wednesday we saw something called the Tuileries gardens. They were pretty enough, if you like that sort of thing.

On Thursday we went to the Louvre and saw the *Mona Lisa*. We'd never been big on art before, but we did find the woman in the painting's smile interesting, although Rebecca did get a funny look from the museum guard when she wondered aloud what the woman would look like with a dark mustache inked under her nose. It probably didn't help when Rebecca started asking if anyone had a pen.

On Friday we saw the Eiffel Tower, but even though Uncle George offered to take us up in it, none of us wanted to go. Looking up at it—how high it was! how narrow at the top!—all of us, even Annie, began to feel dizzy. We'd never suffered from vertigo before, the fear of heights, but we suspected such a thing could come upon a person suddenly and with no warning.

Those were the days. As for the nights and all those parties, although we saw different sights each day, the nights were all the same: Rebecca cornering Crazy Serena, us hearing fragments of Rebecca's questions and accusations—"Frank Freud . . . the Wicket"—and then hearing Crazy Serena call Rebecca "wretched child."

We admired Rebecca for choosing a goal and sticking to it—something other than suggesting our parents might be dead each time one of us mentioned their disappearance—but it didn't look to us like she was getting anywhere in the getting-the-truth-out-of-Crazy-Serena program.

Sometimes we wondered if we'd ever get the truth

about anything, or if there even were any great truths to be had.

One other thing that was the same about those nights: Petal under the bed.

Some bad things, we realized, never changed.

* * * * * * * *

And then it was Saturday, the day of the wedding of Aunt Martha to Uncle George.

It was a gorgeous day, the kind of day we imagined every bride dreamed of, even though we couldn't imagine ourselves dreaming of a wedding day. The sky was a blue crystal with little puffy white clouds, and the very air smelled like every flower in the world, only not too strong, which would have been annoying.

Aunt Martha looked gorgeous in her gown and veil when she came by to ask us to wish her luck before the ceremony. It was to take place in one of the chateau's two ballrooms, and the reception afterward would take place in the other.

As for us, we may not have been wearing floor-length gowns with huge trains trailing behind us, but in our party dresses and accompanied by our cats, we thought we looked pretty spiffy too.

It would all have been so perfect, if only . . .

"Please come out from under there," Aunt Martha begged, getting down on the floor, gown and all.

We realized it then: for a relative, she was a genuinely nice woman.

"I don't want to get married without you there," Aunt Martha went on.

"You barely knew us before this week," the muffled voice said.

"I know," Aunt Martha admitted, "but now I can't imagine my life without you. And I certainly can't imagine getting married without you, without *all of you* there. It must be so awful for George. I don't mean about marrying me, but doing so without Queen and Lucy by his side. I mean, I think we can all acknowledge that Serena is hardly a consolation prize."

She had a point there, although we were still confused. Who was Queen, and what did she have to do with everyone else?

"C'mon," Annie said to Petal. "Don't disappoint Aunt Martha."

"We can't afford to get a nice relative mad at us," Durinda said.

"Keep doing that—" Georgia started.

"—and we won't have anyone left," Jackie finished.

"Does anyone else ever think," Marcia commented, "that the only purpose we all serve in the others' life stories is to help the person who's in the spotlight at the moment become the best version of herself she can be?"

"No." Rebecca rolled her eyes. "No one thinks that. No one in the whole world thinks that."

"You have to come, Petal," Zinnia said. "I think I'm going to have a Big Moment today with these flowers, and it won't mean half so much without you there."

"C'mon," Annie said again. "If you come down to the wedding, I won't try to stop you if you want to spend the whole time with your eyes squinched shut babbling *weiofyoihfaifihweiw*. But please don't spoil the day for Aunt Martha."

"Ohhhhhh, *fine*." Petal at last consented.

* * * * * * * *

Large crowd made up mostly of strangers. Organist playing old-fashioned songs. Frilly lace-edged white socks that kept slipping down our ankles.

Not exactly our idea of a good time, but Aunt Martha looked happy enough as she stood beyond the entrance of the aisle some way behind Zinnia.

"Oh, I wish Mommy and Daddy could be here," Annie said.

"It seems wrong, them not being here," Durinda said.

"I know," Georgia said. "It's Daddy's sister waiting to come in."

"And Mommy's brother waiting for her in front of the altar," Jackie said.

"It's too bad they both disappeared when they did," Marcia said.

"*Yugfawliuefa,*" Petal said.

Then a disturbing silence occurred, and we don't mean the pause before the Wedding March. It was the silence created by Rebecca *not* saying "or died," given what Marcia had said before Petal had said "*Yugfawliuefa.*"

We all looked around us, filling with a worry and dread worthy of Petal.

Where was Rebecca? We were sure she'd come into the ballroom with us, and yet now she was nowhere to be seen.

"She's missing," Marcia said, "but there's someone else I don't see in the room either."

As soon as she said it, we saw she was right.

Crazy Serena wasn't in the room.

"Maybe she went to the bathroom?" Durinda suggested.

"I don't think that's where Crazy Serena is," Jackie said, "although she is in France."

"I don't think it's a coincidence they're both not here," Georgia said. "I have the feeling something evil is going on." Georgia knew something about evil.

"Do you think Crazy Serena has abducted her?" Petal finally piped up, having opened her eyes and ceased to babble.

"That's exactly what I think," Annie said gravely. "I think Crazy Serena has taken Rebecca, for whatever reason, and the only way to get her back is for you to use your power. Read Crazy Serena's mind. Figure out where she's taken Rebecca and what she plans to do with her. *Read her mind, Petal.* Please."

Petal reeled back in horror at the very idea of using her power to peer into the dark reaches of Crazy Serena's crazy little mind.

But then Petal did something we could never have imagined her doing, not in a million years.

She stopped reeling backward and instead came forward, forcefully.

"Stop the wedding!" she shouted.

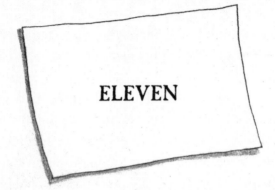

ELEVEN

Okay, it was a little melodramatic, we grant you that. But who could blame Petal? Her sister had been abducted. Her aunt had done the abducting. How could a wedding take place until we got Rebecca safely back?

But hang on here.

Did we really want her back? Hmmm . . .

Oh. Right. Of course we did.

We looked at Petal and couldn't quite believe what we were seeing, what we were hearing.

In the history of the universe, no Huit had ever been more likely to refuse the call to adventure than Petal. She'd already refused it once, when she refused her power after its arrival, and we'd assumed she'd go on refusing it throughout eternity, and what sort of person does that? Maybe Georgia had once refused her gift when it arrived too early, but none of us, not even contrary Georgia, would refuse her power. Except for Petal.

And yet now . . .

"No one in our family," Petal spoke clearly, "has tormented me for as long or with such glee as Rebecca. She's made me feel stupid and she's made me feel small. But none of that matters now. She's *my sister*. I have to do this, no matter how much it scares me."

And then Petal tilted her head at an angle and began spinning around slowly as though she were leaving no stone unturned in her quest to read Crazy Serena's mind, as though she were trying to catch the frequency of all of France.

"Got anything yet?" Georgia wondered.

"She's still tilting and spinning," Annie said in a hushed voice.

"Now?" Georgia wondered. "Anything?"

"Shush," Durinda shushed. "She needs to concentrate."

"How's it going over here?" Pete asked, drawing closer, Mrs. Pete next to him. "Any—"

"Got it!" Petal cried, and please let us say here that a Petal triumphant was a glorious thing to see.

"Where, pet?" Pete said urgently. "Where is she?"

"Oh no." The triumph in Petal's eyes had died and she was back to looking horrified. "Crazy Serena's got Rebecca and she's taking her to the top of the Eiffel Tower . . . and she's thinking of throwing her over the side!"

* * * * * * * *

There were no taxis outside the chateau, we saw as we raced outside after Pete, Zinnia still clutching her basket of rose petals.

But there was a long limo, the one that was waiting to take Aunt Martha and Uncle George on their honeymoon.

"The Eiffel Tower, my good man," Pete directed the startled limo driver as seven Eights plus eights cats and the Petes piled in. "And step on it, please. We've got a little person to save."

That was enough for the limo driver, and he didn't even complain about the cats.

"Don't worry," Zinnia soothed Rambunctious, who was in her lap along with Zither. "We'll get to Rebecca in time."

The way that limo driver sped through the French countryside and into the city, you'd think the limo was a plane instead of a car; he got us to our destination in no time.

"Wait here for us, please," Pete directed as we all tore out of the limo so fast we left the doors hanging open behind us.

We had to hand it to Pete as we raced after him. Even in times of trouble he had good manners, remembering to say *please* to the limo driver like that.

At the base of the Eiffel Tower we stopped long enough to stare up at its terrifying height. We gulped at the thought of going to the top.

But then Petal rallied us to battle.

"Come on," she said. "We need to hurry. I just read Crazy Serena's mind, and she was thinking, 'In another few minutes, I'll never have to hear wretched Rebecca ask me another annoying question ever again.'"

We hurried, going up the Eiffel Tower until we came out onto the observation deck at the top.

Boy, it was windy.

"Stop right there!" Pete shouted, pointing an accusing finger at Crazy Serena as she heaved a bound Rebecca up in her arms and moved to the edge.

We did notice that Pete neglected to say *please* this time.

Crazy Serena turned to us, a nervous smile on her face.

"I wasn't going to do anything evil," she said, "really. We were just playing Mother and Child. It's a game we made up together. Tell them, Rebecca."

But Rebecca was saying nothing except *"Whgfauvuwe,"* which she mumbled in a funny sort of way because there was a sock shoved in her mouth.

We were fairly certain we knew who had put that sock there.

"Step away from the edge and put the child down," Pete directed in a calm but firm voice.

Immediately, and to our great surprise, Crazy Serena obeyed.

But then we figured: Of course she did. Who would ever argue with a calm but firm mechanic?

"Now tell me why you did it," Pete said. "Why did you abduct Rebecca and why were you about to throw her over the side?"

"I already told you," Crazy Serena insisted. "I wasn't—"

"'Because Rebecca wouldn't stop asking me questions and she was driving me crazy, so I had to find a way to get her to stop,'" Petal piped up in a disturbingly Crazy Serena–like voice. Petal shrugged. "At least that's what was in her mind just then."

Crazy Serena studied Petal, stunned. "One of you can read people's minds now?" she said in a wondering voice. "What are you—a witch?"

"No, that would be you," Rebecca said right after Annie untied her and removed the sock from her mouth.

"Is it true?" Pete asked Crazy Serena. "Is that what you were thinking?"

Crazy Serena looked at him with pleading eyes. "It's exactly true. But surely you understand, don't you? Haven't you ever had a child pepper you with the same annoying questions over and over again so that you feel if you can't keep the kid quiet you'll go mad?"

"No," Pete said wearily. "I can't say as I've ever had that particular experience and I don't imagine I ever will."

Then he closed the space between them, grabbed her firmly by the elbow, and led her down the Eiffel Tower, the rest of us trailing behind.

When we got to the bottom, in a move we'd seen him make one time before, he gave her a slight push on the back, like he was starting a wind-up toy.

"One more time," he said. "Off you go. Get out of France. I kicked you out of one country and now I'm kicking you out of another. And if it comes to it, I'll kick you out of every country on the planet. Just stay away from my girls!"

It was an odd thing for him to say, we thought as we watched Crazy Serena hobble off, but then we realized: for however long our parents were gone, we were Pete's girls, and we were grateful for it.

"Thank you, Mr. Pete!" Rebecca hurled herself at him and gave him a big hug. "You saved me."

For the first time we realized that Rebecca, who'd never seemed to know what *fear* meant, had been scared.

"Anytime, pet," Pete said. "And I appreciate the appreciation. But you need to thank Petal for this one."

"*Petal?*" Rebecca spat out the name with her usual level of disgust.

"Yes," Pete said evenly. "Petal. She's the one who grew brave enough to use her power to read Crazy Serena's mind. If not for her, we'd never have known where to look for you. I doubt we'd have gotten here in time."

As frustrating as it was sometimes to have Rebecca for a sister, that was an awful thought.

"Petal?" Rebecca turned to Petal, confusion and wonder in her voice. "But I don't understand. I've treated you horribly since we were born. Why would you do anything to save me? You should hate me."

"You're my sister." Petal shrugged. "Who would I be if I didn't save you?"

"But weren't you scared?" Rebecca went on. "Weren't you worried that the sky would fall or that it would rain for forty days and forty nights or that the world would just generally come to an end?"

"Of course I was scared, of all those things," Petal said. "I always am. I was scared every single second, for myself. But you're my sister. You're my sister."

And then, of course, Petal fainted.

* * * * * * * *

"Gather her up and let's get going," Mrs. Pete said cheerily. "We've got a wedding to get to."

Back at the chateau, now that Crazy Serena was gone, the wedding went off without a hitch. You could even say it was boring, although it was a nice moment when Petal bravely took the basket with its few remaining

rose petals from Zinnia, and Zinnia graciously allowed
her to be the one to strew the aisle with them.

But then—once Aunt Martha and Uncle George had
each said "I do" and kissed and we'd all had the chance
to say, "Euwww!"—at the reception in the second ballroom things got exciting again.

We had never been to a wedding reception before,
so we didn't know there'd be a table set up with little
cards on it, each card with the name of a guest and an
assigned table number.

It relieved us greatly to see that we and the Petes would all be at the same table together: table 8.

But then we started looking at the other name cards waiting to be claimed and we saw that nearly every card there was for a person with the last name Smith.

Huh. Who would have ever guessed there were so many people named Smith in the world?

Then we shrugged. They must all be relatives of Mommy.

We began scanning the cards to see if there were any non-Smith names, just out of curiosity.

That's when we saw one still there for Serena Smith.

"Sorry," Uncle George said, reaching over us. "Someone should have removed this earlier. Sorry again." He shook his head. "Serena's always been a bad egg."

We glanced at Rebecca out of the corners of our eyes. We knew all about bad eggs, because we had one of our own. Still, we loved our bad egg.

"Oh, hello!" Uncle George cried. "What are these doing still here? They're not coming."

We saw him hurriedly gather up about ten more cards. Before he put them in his pocket, we noticed that the top one said *Ocho*. Then we heard the sound of knives clinking against glasses, and Uncle George went off to kiss Aunt Martha again.

Euwww.

"Ocho?" Rebecca said. "Hmm . . . I remember that

from the Spanish words the Mr. McG tried to teach us. It means 'eight.'"

Eight? In Spanish? But that was odd. Our name meant "eight" in French.

"Never mind that now," Annie said, struggling under the weight of the Deluxe Perfect-Every-Time Hamburger Maker/Manicure-Pedicure Machine that she was carrying on her head. "Can we go find the presents table so I can put this down before it squashes me?"

We shrugged and followed behind her.

That's another thing they have at wedding receptions. In addition to the name-card table, there's a presents table.

We had no idea when such information might come in handy again, but most of us did think it was nice to know things.

"Ooh!" Zinnia clasped her hands together at the sight of all the pretty wrapped presents.

"Oof!" Annie exhaled, relieved to finally set our present down.

"Can we look at some of these before we find our seats?" Zinnia begged. "Please?"

"Suit yourselves." Annie waved an exhausted hand. Then she grabbed a napkin from a table that wasn't ours and wiped her brow.

We proceeded to ooh and aah over the packages,

even those of us who weren't as obsessed with presents as others were. It was a wedding, and it seemed like another wedding thing people did.

We also studied the names on the gift cards to see who'd brought what, but we didn't see the names of anyone we knew, save on the card with practical cash inside it from the Petes.

"Look at that one in the back!" Zinnia said. "So big! So shiny!"

"I wonder who it's from?" Jackie wondered.

"We probably shouldn't—" Annie started to say as Zinnia strained to pull the big and shiny package from the back row. "Oh, here," Annie said instead, exasperated. "Let me get that for you. I am seven inches taller, you know."

Yes. We did know.

Annie looked over each shoulder to see if anyone else was looking before she reached, grabbed. "I just hope no one notices—" Then she saw something attached to the package that brought her up short.

It brought *all* of us up short.

"Hello! What's this?" Annie said.

But we could all see what it was.

It was a gift card with the words *So sorry to miss your special day—regrets from the Ochos!*

"There's that name again," Annie said, puzzled.

"The same as on those name cards Uncle George took away," Durinda said.

"Hmm," Georgia said.

"Perhaps we should ask Uncle George about it?" Petal piped up. We'd noticed that since saving Rebecca she'd grown somewhat bolder.

"Good idea," Jackie said.

So that's what we did.

"Uncle George, I am curious," Marcia said. It was natural for her to be the one to ask, since she was the curious type, that scientific mind of hers and all. "Who are the Ochos?"

Uncle George blinked at us. "You can't be serious."

"Oh, but we are," Rebecca said darkly, then added for emphasis, "*very* serious."

"Well," he said, "Queen married Joe Ocho—"

"Joe Ocho?" Zinnia laughed. "What a name!"

"I agree," Uncle George said, "but you can't really pick what you were named, just like you can't pick your relatives, so I never say anything to him about it."

"But who is Queen?" Annie asked.

There was that blinking look from Uncle George again. "Don't you know anything about your own family? Why, Queen is Lucy's identical twin sister. She's *your* mother's twin."

What?

Then someone started banging a knife against a glass, which we'd figured out was the way guests let Uncle George know they wanted to see him kiss Aunt Martha again.

Euwww.

"Uncle George!" Annie shouted after him. "Do Queen and Joe Ocho have any kids?"

"Of course!" Uncle George shouted back to us. "They have—"

But whatever number he said was drowned out by the increased volume of knife-glass clinking.

We froze where we were, then slowly swiveled our heads, looking at one another.

Our last name was Huit, meaning "eight" in French.

Queen and Joe's last name was Ocho, meaning "eight" in Spanish.

And Queen and Joe Ocho had some children, number unspecified.

Could their children be the other Eights?

TWELVE

We didn't learn anything further about the Ochos on that trip. Aunt Martha and Uncle George were too busy being just-married people to answer any more of our questions, and then they were off-on-their-honeymoon people, so they weren't even there to answer them. As for the rest of the guests, we'd done nothing to get to know them, had we? And it probably didn't help matters any that Petal had been babbling things like *uegfyaiugfwfgi* for most of the week and then had shrieked, *"Stop the wedding!"* Neither of which, we realized, was likely to endear us to new people.

But that was okay. Petal had saved Rebecca, and that was enough. We'd learn the truth, or not, when the time came.

* * * * * * * *

We spent Sunday seeing more sights, and to an Eight we decided, "We *love* France!"

Then it was Monday, time for us to head home.

The flight back was uneventful. No one tried to fly us to a different country because he or she was missing a relative, for which we were grateful.

Conflict and tension had their places, we realized, but sometimes we needed a break.

Arriving home, we said goodbye and thank you to the Petes, kissed Daddy Sparky and Mommy Sally, and said hi to Carl the talking refrigerator.

"Eggs have gone rotten in your absence," Carl informed us, "but robot Betty still loves Carl, so all is right in Carl's world." Then we could swear the talking refrigerator smiled at us when he added, "Glad you're back."

We were glad to be back too. It had been the perfect kind of time away: a trip you are glad to go on and glad to return from. We'd even learned a new fact or two. Sort of.

Of course the cats were ecstatic to be back. They raced one another to go play in Summer. We knew they'd missed the seasonal rooms a lot, as did we, and we only hoped they didn't try to use the sand in there as one big litter box.

We did notice Precious giving Rambunctious funny looks, and we wondered what evil things Rambunctious was thinking.

Then we shrugged. A little over a week from now both Petal's and Precious's powers would go to sleep, at least sort of, which would probably make the both of them a lot happier.

We were on our way to the staircase to go upstairs and unpack right away—Annie's orders—when Precious came in with a shiny silver object. She dropped it in Petal's hand and then disappeared back into Summer.

"What's that?" Georgia asked.

"It looks like a charm bracelet," Petal said.

"Of course it's a charm bracelet." Rebecca was back to sneering. "It's a silver bracelet and it has charms. What else could it be?"

"It must be your gift," Jackie said.

"I wish it were mine," Zinnia said.

"Petal," Durinda said, "go see if there's a new note in the wall for you."

We all went.

The usual loose stone in the drawing room was slightly pulled away from the wall, and when Petal pulled it out entirely, she did indeed find a note behind it. The note read:

Dear Petal,

Twelve down, four to go. Nice job being so brave—I do realize this has been particularly hard on you.

"And how," Petal said to the note.

As always, the note was unsigned.

It also didn't answer Petal back.

"Those notes are simply amazing," Marcia observed. "They find us in the house, they find us in France. Whoever writes them must be incredibly resourceful, a real Jim Dandy. Hmm . . . I wonder if a note would find us in Antarctica or on the moon?"

"I wouldn't want to find out," Annie said.

"Well, I would," Georgia said wistfully. "I think either place would be fun."

"Who wants a snack after we unpack?" Durinda said.

"I do!" Zinnia said.

"Will you need help with that, Durinda?" Jackie offered.

"Thank you," Durinda said.

We started up the stairs in a line.

"I'm just looking forward to a week from tomorrow," Petal said.

"A week from tomorrow?" Annie echoed. "But why?"

"Because a week from tomorrow it'll be July," Petal said happily, "and then I mostly won't have to worry about my power anymore."

"Wait a second," Annie said slowly, which was odd. Annie was never slow about anything. "If your month ends a week from tomorrow with the start of July, then it also means that a week from tomorrow is . . ."

She let the horrifying notion drift off uncompleted as we all slowly turned and looked at Rebecca, who was standing at the end of the line, even behind Zinnia.

"Yesssss." Rebecca dragged the word out, her eyes flashing darkly. "That's when my month begins."

The idea of Rebecca having her own month, of Rebecca having a power.

Was it too early, we wondered, to prepare . . .

"Run!" seven Eights shouted.

And then we raced up the stairs and dived under our beds.

Don't miss any of the stories of the Sisters Eight!

And coming soon:
REBECCA'S RASHNESS